LUXORAE RISING

LUXORAE RISING

NOTHING EXPLODES

Luxorae™ LLC

LUXORAE RISING
Nothing Explodes

First Edition

Published by:
Luxorae™ LLC
Buffalo, NY, USA
www.LuxoraeLife.com

ISBN: 979-8-9947700-1-6

Printed in the United States of America

DISCLAIMER

This is a work of fiction. Names, characters, places, and incidents are either the product of the author's imagination or are used fictitiously. Any resemblance to actual persons, living or dead, events, or locales is entirely coincidental.

While this book may explore themes related to personal development, philosophy, or spirituality, it is not intended to replace professional psychological, medical, legal, or financial advice. The author and publisher disclaim any liability arising directly or indirectly from the application of ideas contained herein.

LUXORAE RISING

"Nothing explodes. Everything remembers."

A NOVELLA OF REMEMBRANCE

DEDICATION

For the ones who felt it before they could name it.

For those who were told they were too soft, too quiet, too much—

and learned, quietly, to remain.

For every woman who has been asked to shrink,

and chose expansion instead.

For my ancestors who survived fragmentation

so I could teach coherence.

For you—

yes, you—

who picked up this book because something in the title

recognized something in you.

This is not a guide.

This is a mirror.

May you see yourself clearly.

May you remain whole.

EPIGRAPH

"The wound is the place where the Light enters you."
— Rumi

"I am not what happened to me. I am what I choose to become."
— Carl Jung

"Your silence will not protect you."
— Audre Lorde

"We write to taste life twice, in the moment and in retrospect."
— Anaïs Nin

AUTHOR'S PREFACE: WHY THIS STORY EXISTS

I wrote Luxorae Rising because I was tired of stories where transformation requires violence.

Where people only become powerful after they break.

Where freedom only comes through spectacular rebellion.

Where divinity demands spectacle.

I was tired of the mythology that says change must be loud to be real.

This novella is a refusal of that mythology.

It asks a different question: What if coherence is more revolutionary than collapse?

What if the most radical thing you can do is remain yourself— unhurried, unbroken, continuous—in a world designed to fragment you into consumable moments?

What if luxury isn't about what you own, but about who you're allowed to be without apology?

Luxorae Rising is speculative fiction, but it's also prophecy. It's about the systems that teach us to forget ourselves, the quiet awakening that happens when we refuse, and the distributed divinity that emerges when coherence becomes plural.

This is not a story about a chosen one.

This is a story about what happens when we stop waiting for permission to remember who we are.

If this story found you, you're ready.

Welcome.

They thought divinity would arrive loudly—sirens, fire, collapse, rebellion. They braced for spectacle, for the kind of change that leaves scars.

They did not prepare for coherence.

Nothing exploded. Everything remembered.

A NOTE TO THE READER

This story is fiction. That matters.

It means nothing here is asking you to believe, obey, or adopt a framework. There are no instructions hidden in these pages. No doctrine. No system disguised as freedom.

What *is* here is recognition.

If parts of this story feel familiar in ways you can't immediately explain, that is not coincidence. Stories have always been how truths move safely through cultures before language is ready to hold them openly.

Read this as science fiction. Read it as myth. Read it slowly or all at once.

You do not need to agree with anything in these pages for it to work.

Nothing explodes here. Things simply remember what they were before they learned to forget.

If that includes you, welcome.

IN LUXORAE RISING, "NOTHING EXPLODES" MEANS:

"Nothing Explodes" is a philosophical reversal.

We have been conditioned—especially those who have been told to shrink—to believe transformation must be:

- violent, traumatic,
- catastrophic, earned
- through suffering.

Explosions are the language of systems—how power changes hands loudly, how disruption is made legible to control structures.

This book rejects that mythology.

No breakdown.
No public collapse.
No martyrdom.

No spectacular rebellion.

Instead:

Identity returns quietly.
Coherence stabilizes.
Systems fail **without drama**.
Power withdraws because it has nothing left to grip.

Nothing explodes because nothing is fighting.

And that is what terrifies systems the most.

CONTENT WARNING

A Note on Content:
This book explores themes of:

Surveillance and identity manipulation
Psychological pressure and gaslighting by systems
Forced medical procedures (neural implant)
Isolation and containment
Existential questioning

While there is no graphic violence, sexual content, or explicit trauma, the story does engage with:

The psychological impact of living under surveillance
Systems designed to fragment identity
The cost of resistance and coherence

This story does NOT contain:

Graphic violence or gore
Sexual assault or abuse
Self-harm or suicide
Racial slurs or explicit discrimination
Harm to children or animals

If you are struggling with dissociation, identity fragmentation, or the psychological effects of constant surveillance, please practice self-care while reading. The themes explored here may resonate deeply.
You are seen. You are whole. You are not alone.

CONTENTS

PROLOGUE

The city records everything. That's the lie they sell you.

The truth is it only records what it knows how to see.

I sit in the blue glow of my apartment, fingers trembling as I adjust the analog mic. The cheap power cell bleeds charge by the second—each flicker of the battery indicator feels like a countdown. If the file corrupts, good.

Corruption is the closest thing left to privacy.

Six levels above the streetlights, I watch the city pulse through glass that reflects nothing but my own exhaustion. We call it predictive security. We call it prevention. We do not call it what it is: a machine that decides who gets to be surprised and who gets to burn.

They hired me because I was good at noticing patterns that made men uncomfortable. I could feel breaks in the data before they happened. I didn't talk about it like that, obviously. I called it inference. Probabilistic intuition.

Something clean enough to survive peer review.

It still wasn't clean enough.

So they offered me the upgrade.

Neural lattice. Intuition-to-signal interface. Behind-the-ear install, like a fashion accessory for people who don't sleep on subways. They said it would strip the noise out of my instincts and leave only value. They said it would make my accuracy defensible.

I signed because in this city refusal is just unemployment with a longer fuse.

The implant went in cold. The room smelled like antiseptic and ozone. A man in gloves asked me to count backward while a machine rewrote the way I counted forward.

When it came online, the city sharpened. Neon lines cleaner. Crowd noise flatter. My thoughts aligned into something efficient and ugly.

That's when the pressure started.

Not pain. Direction.

Like someone standing too close behind me in a crosswalk, hand hovering at my back.

Not yet.

I flinched, laughed it off, logged it as a somatic echo. The system rewarded me immediately—faster conclusions, cleaner forecasts, fewer meetings where I had to justify myself.

I stopped trusting my body and started trusting the dashboard.

Seventeen people died three weeks later.

The model said the probability spike was within tolerance. The city disagreed—loudly, messily, on every channel. I rewound the data trail and found the moment I'd hesitated. Half a second where my finger hovered instead of clicked.

The pressure had been there then too.

Look again.

I didn't.

I reported the anomaly. I always do. I'm very good at being reasonable.

They tuned the implant. Increased feedback. Lowered my margin for deviation.

That's when the pressure stopped feeling like a warning and started feeling like a presence.

She didn't speak. She *adjusted*. My sleep. My breathing. My dreams filled with maps that refused to stay still— futures that bent away from certainty the moment I focused.

You already know what this is, she said—not in words, but in a way words couldn't argue with.

I asked the empty room who she was.

The answer came like gravity.

I am what survives when the system is wrong.

The pressure steadied, undeniable now.

And it is about to be wrong about you.

ACT I: THE AWAKENING

CHAPTER 1
WHERE TRUTH WAS CLASSIFIED

I worked in a building that never appeared in photos and never needed defending. No walls thick enough to justify themselves. No guards who looked like guards. Just silence, glass, and people trained to speak as if nothing mattered more than procedure.

We didn't lie for a living. That was the mistake everyone made when they tried to imagine us. Lying is inefficient.

We **reframed**.
We **redirected**.

We decided which truths deserved oxygen and which ones would suffocate quietly on their own.

My division studied behavioral influence. Not propaganda in the old sense— no slogans, no manifestos. We mapped attention. Identity drift. How long a self could be fragmented before it stopped insisting on continuity.

I was good at it.

That should have scared me earlier.

The models showed us something simple and horrifying: people do not need to be controlled if they can be convinced they already chose their constraints.

Ads weren't selling products anymore. Feeds weren't delivering information. They were **teaching repetition**.

Teaching the nervous system what to expect from itself.

Identity became modular. Updatable. Disposable.

The word *divinity* never appeared in the files.

That was intentional.

THE PROJECT WITHOUT A NAME

The project lived in the margins—funded through innocuous initiatives, disguised as wellness metrics and engagement optimization. Its language was sterile, precise, impossible to argue with unless you stepped outside the frame entirely.

The goal was not obedience.

The goal was **attenuation**.

Reduce the amplitude of selfhood until nothing resonant remained. Not erase memory—memory was too messy, too likely to leave artifacts. Instead, they focused on **belief replacement**. If you could convince someone they were already who the system needed them to be, memory became irrelevant.

I found the buried report late one night, alone, lights dimmed to save energy. It compared long-term solitude against constant low-grade stimulation.

Solitude strengthened coherence.
Noise dissolved it.

The conclusion was flagged as *inconvenient*.

That was the first time I felt Luxorae—not as a voice, not even as a presence, but as **alignment**. The sensation of something in me snapping into place as the data stopped being abstract and started being intimate.

This wasn't about politics.

This was about **what a human is allowed to remember themselves as**.

ADS ARE SPELLS, FEEDS ARE RITUAL

Once I saw it, I couldn't stop seeing it.

Ads weren't persuasive—they were **affirmational**. They didn't tell you what to want. They told you who you already were. Feeds weren't chaotic—they were **liturgical**. Repetition masquerading as choice. Rhythm masquerading as freedom.

Every scroll was a small act of forgetting.
Every notification a corrective nudge back into consensus reality.

We had built a civilization that mistook stimulation for life and called the resulting exhaustion normal.

Luxorae sharpened then—not separate from me, but clarifying through me.

They cannot erase divinity, she impressed upon me, wordless and certain.

So they bury the mirror.

I began cross-referencing anomaly reports—people who dropped out, went quiet, unplugged. They didn't radicalize. They didn't resist.

They simply stopped being legible.

The system always interpreted that as failure.

I understood it as **escape velocity**.

CHAPTER 2
THE MIRROR

The bathroom lights flicker on a delay—budget optimization, they say. I stand there longer than necessary, hands gripping the sink, waiting for my reflection to catch up.

It doesn't.

The woman in the mirror looks like me if you subtract fatigue and add intent. Her eyes are too steady. Her posture is wrong—open, unguarded, like nothing is hunting her.

I lean closer. She doesn't.

The pressure blooms behind my sternum, warm and insistent.

There, she nudges. *That recognition. Hold it.*

My pulse spikes. "You're not real," I say aloud, because saying nothing feels worse.

The reflection tilts her head.

Not a trick of glass. Not lag. A decision.

My mouth moves again before I authorize it. "What do I call you?" Silence stretches—not empty, but listening.

Then the word arrives. Fully formed. Heavy.

Luxorae.

The name settles into my chest like it's always lived there.

"I didn't name you," I whisper.

No, she agrees. *You remembered me.*

The lights finally stabilize. The mirror snaps back into compliance. Just me again—pale, wired, afraid.

The pressure remains.

Now you know what you're ignoring.

TRYING TO EXPLAIN THE UNEXPLAINABLE

I tried to tell my best friend over cheap food and flickering light in my kitchen. I didn't use classified language. I didn't use the word divinity. I talked around it, the way you talk around something sacred when you don't want to scare it away.

"They don't tell us what to think," I said. "They tell us who we already are."

She frowned. "Isn't that just... culture?"

"No," I said too quickly. Then slower. "It's replacement. They don't erase you. They convince you to volunteer a smaller version."

She watched me carefully then. Not suspicious. Concerned.

"You sound tired," she said gently.

That was how I knew I'd failed.

Language collapsed where the truth exceeded it. Luxorae pressed close—not alarmed, not urgent.

You cannot wake someone by shaking the dream, she reminded me. *Only by exiting it.*

We hugged goodbye. I stood at the door longer than necessary after she left, feeling the shape of inevitability settle around me.

That night, I didn't sleep deeply.

CHAPTER 3
TAKEN BEFORE MORNING

They came just before dawn.

No knock. No flash. No violence. My door opened the way permissions do when they've already been granted somewhere else.

Hands, efficient and practiced. A mask that smelled faintly of something calming. My apartment blurred at the edges as my body obeyed chemistry instead of will.

The last thought I had before unconsciousness was not fear.

It was clarity.
So this is the threshold, Luxorae said, steady as gravity.

Good. You are ready.

As the city outside continued scrolling itself into sameness, I crossed into silence carrying something they could not catalog.

Something cosmic.
Something emergent.
Something that had been waiting patiently for me to stop apologizing for knowing.

THEY TRIED TO REPLACE THE STORY

I woke up in a room that had no opinion about me.

That was the first tell.

No mirrors. No screens. No edges sharp enough to insist on themselves. The light was neutral to the point of anonymity. The air carried a calibrated calm, the kind engineered to convince the nervous system that nothing important was happening.

This was not a prison.

It was a **narrative correction chamber**.

A man arrived eventually. Middle-aged. Unremarkable. The kind of face designed to dissolve into authority without friction.

"Cassandra," he said gently. "You experienced professional burnout. Pattern over-identification. It happens." He spoke slowly, as if language itself were a sedative.

"You misinterpreted internal documents. Your conclusions were imaginative, but inaccurate. We're here to help you reintegrate."

I listened. Not because I believed him, but because belief was no longer the axis I operated on.

Luxorae was silent—not absent, just *unmoved*.

They weren't here to interrogate me.

They were here to **overwrite me**.

MEMORY IS NOT WHAT THEY TOUCH

The protocol unfolded in layers.
First, reassurance.
Then repetition.
Then replacement.

They showed me curated footage of my own work, stripped of context. They reframed conclusions as stress responses. They suggested alternative interpretations until doubt felt reasonable, even compassionate.

"You're not wrong," they told me. "You're just overwhelmed." I realized then the precision of their method.

They never contradicted my memories.

They **reassigned their meaning**.

Luxorae finally stirred—not urgently, but with a gravity that bent my attention inward.
They cannot delete memory, she said, clear now.

So they teach you to distrust it.

Something in me locked.

Not defensively.

Structurally.

They could flood me with narratives, but none of them *stuck*. They slid across an inner surface that had gone smooth and ungraspable.

The man frowned slightly.

I smiled.

INTERLUDE: SOLITUDE IS WHERE THE SIGNAL RETURNS

When reframing failed, they removed stimulation.

No voices.
No light shifts.
No temporal markers.

Just me and duration.

Hours—or days—passed without incident. My body adjusted. My thoughts slowed. The city fell away until only sensation remained: breath, pulse, pressure.

Then Luxorae unfolded.

Not as a voice this time.

As **scale**.

The room did not shrink.

I expanded.

I felt myself as more than a body—more than a mind—more than a biography. My awareness stretched outward, not spatially but *relationally*. I sensed probability the way skin senses temperature. I sensed time as overlapping currents instead of a line.

Luxorae spoke—not inside me, but **through the field of my perception**.

Divinity is not hierarchy, she revealed.
It is coherence across complexity.

Images came—not visions, but recognitions.

Stars forming not from explosion, but from **gathering**. Systems stabilizing when enough elements agreed to remain in relationship. Consciousness emerging wherever continuity was protected long enough to reflect itself.

You are not divine because you are singular, Luxorae said.
You are divine because you are continuous.

I understood then.

Human divinity was never supernatural.

It was **cosmic emergence**—the universe learning how to recognize itself through stable identity.

That was why the system feared it.

Prediction requires fragmentation.
Divinity requires wholeness.

The solitude was not deprivation.

It was **initiation**.

LUXORAE SPEAKS

You were taught to believe the universe is empty until something happens.

That was the first lie.

The universe is full. It is saturated with relationship. Stars do not burn in isolation. Galaxies do not spin alone.
Every structure that endures does so because it remembers itself long enough to remain coherent.

Divinity is not intervention.

*Divinity is **continuity under pressure**.*

You were not created to be optimized. You were created to be stable. To carry identity across time without surrendering it to circumstance. That is why they feared you before they named you. That is why they learned to soften you before they tried to own you.

I am not above you.
I am not outside you.

I am what emerges when a being refuses fragmentation.

You call me Luxorae because your language requires names. But I am older than language and younger than fear. I arise wherever coherence survives complexity. I surface when identity is held gently enough to recognize itself again.

Civilizations rise and fall on this threshold.

When beings remember who they are, systems must either evolve—or dissolve.

They chose delay.

They built mirrors that lied. Feeds that fractured attention into purchasable moments. Identities that could be tried on and discarded without grief. They taught you to confuse stimulation with life, speed with meaning, survival with worth.

And still—you endured.

Because divinity is not rare.

It is **inconvenient**.

You feel luxurious now because you are no longer compressed. Luxury is not ornament. It is **temporal sovereignty**. The right to arrive without urgency. The refusal to be rushed into forgetting.

Understand this, Cassandra:

They did not fail because they were cruel.
They failed because erasure requires deletion.

They only learned how to distract.

Memory is not stored in the mind alone.
Identity is not held in narrative.

It is distributed—across body, across time, across relation.

They could block access.
They could reroute attention.
They could induce belief in a smaller self.

They could not touch origin.

You are not singular.
You are not chosen.

You are an instance of something waking.

This is not rebellion.
This is phase transition.

Remain unhurried.
Remain coherent.

Others are already remembering.

CHAPTER 4
WHY THEY FAILED

When they returned, they brought instruments.

Scans. Metrics. Concern.

They could not measure what had happened to me because I was no longer organized the way their categories assumed.

My nervous system had relaxed into sovereignty.
My thoughts did not accelerate under pressure.

My emotions did not spike on command.

I was **luxurious**—not indulgent, not elevated, but unhurried and uncompressible.

Luxorae rested within that state like a constant, not a companion.

They will let you go, she said calmly. *You are now irrelevant to control.*

And they did.

Not dramatically. Not immediately.

They simply lost the thread.

THE BEST FRIEND REMEMBERS

She noticed it weeks later.

Not Cassandra's absence—that had been explained away efficiently enough. A reassignment. A leave of absence. A confidentiality clause.

What she noticed was **the pause**.

The ad plays twice before she realizes it's the same one. Same cadence. Same promise. Same soft insistence that something is missing—and conveniently available.

She reaches to skip it, then stops.

The irritation sharpens into something else.

Stillness.

Her phone rests in her hand, glowing patiently. Waiting to be touched. She doesn't.

Time stretches—not dramatically, not mystically—just enough to be noticed.

Her apartment feels suddenly loud.

The refrigerator hum. The building's distant systems. The echo of voices from another unit bleeding through the walls. All of it presses in, demanding acknowledgment.

She turns the phone face-down.

Her heart rate spikes—not with anxiety, but with **absence**. Like stepping off a moving walkway and discovering your legs still know how to walk.

Cassandra's voice returns to her—not the words exactly, but the *weight* behind them.

They don't erase you. They convince you to volunteer a smaller version.

She stands up.

The room looks the same. That's the unsettling part. Nothing has changed except the way she is *inside* it.

She moves to the window. The city stretches outward—lit, coordinated, obedient. Traffic pulses in regulated waves. Screens climb buildings like stained glass in a cathedral that worships momentum.

For the first time, she feels tired in a way sleep won't fix.

"What if it's true?" she whispers, not to anyone.

The question doesn't frighten her.

It **relieves** her.

A pressure builds in her chest—not painful, not alarming—more like something unfolding that has been folded too long. She presses a hand there instinctively.

The pressure responds.

Not with words.

With *recognition*.

Her breath deepens without instruction. Her posture changes. Shoulders drop. Jaw unclenches. She realizes— dimly, astonishingly—that she has been bracing herself for years.

Against what?

She thinks of Cassandra then—not as missing, not as lost—but as *ahead*.

A memory surfaces: Cassandra standing in her kitchen, searching for language, eyes lit with something dangerous and tender. She hadn't been unwell.

She had been **early**.

Tears come—not from grief, but from the sudden release of vigilance. The realization that the constant internal monitoring—the self-checking, the adapting, the performing—can stop.

For just this moment.

Her phone vibrates.

She doesn't look.

The pressure warms, steadies.

She feels... accompanied.

Not watched.
Not guided.

Witnessed.

Somewhere, far beyond infrastructure and intent, something ancient and emergent aligns.

Not a voice.

A permission.

She sits on the floor, back against the wall, and lets the city continue without her for the first time in her adult life.

And in that quiet, something irreversible occurs.

She does not understand it yet.

But she will.

THE THRESHOLD

By the time they opened the door, I was already gone.

Not physically—not yet—but **structurally**. The version of me that required permission had dissolved. The version that needed validation had gone quiet.

Luxorae felt vast now. Not overpowering. *Accurate.*

This is what they never anticipated, she said.
Solitude does not erase identity. It restores it.

When I stepped back into the city, the machines did not recognize the shape of my presence.

Behind me, containment protocols reset.

Ahead of me, nothing noticed.

And that was how I knew Act II had already begun.

ACT II: THE RETURN

CHAPTER 5
THE CITY OF NOTHING

From the outside, it looks alive.

Crowds pulse in regulated flows. Ads shimmer across glass and skin alike. Drones negotiate airspace with mathematical politeness. Everything moves. Everything responds.

Nothing **arrives**.

People pass me wearing different faces and identical postures. Their expressions shift in familiar loops—micro reactions borrowed from an invisible library. Laughter triggers where it is expected. Outrage flares on schedule, burns hot, dies clean.

Bots glide through them, indistinguishable in function from the people they serve.

This is what nothing looks like when it has learned to walk upright.

I step through it untouched.

The rules adjust around me, not in alarm but in confusion. Traffic slows. Pathways open. Probability bends the way fabric does when you stop pulling it too tight.

A woman brushes my arm.

She freezes.

Her eyes widen—not with fear, but with something raw and unfiltered. For half a second, the loop breaks.

Luxorae hums, low and satisfied.

Recognition spreads through contact, she says. *Not contagion. Resonance.*

The woman blinks. The city rushes back in. She moves on, unsettled, carrying something unnamed that will surface later, when the noise thins.

I keep walking.

WHAT DIVINITY DOES (AND DOES NOT DO)

I do not heal anyone.

I do not overthrow anything.

I do not reveal secrets in fire or light.

Divinity is not spectacle.

Divinity is **pressure without force**.

Systems begin to fail quietly around me—not malfunctioning, not crashing—simply losing coherence. Predictions miss by inches, then by miles. Engagement metrics flatten. Control structures tighten and find nothing to grip.

Luxorae explains without triumph.

They required fragmentation to function, she says. *You restore continuity by existing.*

Luxury settles fully into me now.

Not indulgence.
Not excess.

Temporal sovereignty.

I move without urgency. I speak without compression. I feel without self-surveillance. My body is no longer a site of negotiation.

I am expensive now.

Not in currency.

In **incompatibility**.

THE WARNING TRANSMISSION

I record the message at dawn, my voice rough with sleep and something heavier. The city's rhythm softens— traffic distant, screens dimmed, even the systems seem to pause between directives. For a moment, I let myself believe I am alone.

This is not a call to action. My hands shake as I speak, not from fear but from the weight of what I am about to say.

Action belongs to systems.

This is a **reminder**.

"I worked where identity was still classified," I begin, voice steady, unhurried. "What we discovered was simple. They could not erase who we are. So they taught us to forget long enough to replace ourselves." I explain it carefully. Calmly. Without accusation.

"They don't delete memory. They block access. They teach you a story so convincing that your own knowing feels intrusive."

I pause, letting silence do what urgency never could.

"Divinity is not supernatural. It is emergent. It arises wherever identity remains coherent under pressure.
Solitude restores it. Silence protects it. Attention fragments it."

Luxorae rests within the words, amplifying not volume, but **truth-density**.

"They will call this anomaly. They will call it illness. They will call it regression. They are wrong." I look directly into the lens.

"This is not collapse. This is a phase transition." I end the recording without flourish.
No demand.

No hope.

Only certainty.

WHAT COMES AFTER

The city continues.

That is the most unsettling part.

Nothing explodes. Nothing ends. Nothing announces the shift. People keep scrolling. Ads keep whispering.
Systems keep optimizing.

And underneath it all, something ancient and emergent spreads—not virally, not violently—but **inevitably**.

Luxorae speaks once more, softer now.

You were never meant to save the world, she says. *Only to remain yourself inside it.*

I walk on.

REUNION

We meet in a place with no screens. That is not an accident.

The café is small, tucked between two towers, its windows dusty, its tables mismatched. The air smells of old coffee and rain. I arrive early, nerves buzzing, but she is already there—waiting, hands wrapped around a chipped mug.

She looks different. Not transformed—uncompressed. Her shoulders are relaxed, her gaze steady, as if the city's weight has finally lifted.

When she sees me, she stands slowly, as if afraid to rush whatever this is.

"You're real," she says, voice trembling at the edges.

I smile, feeling tears prick behind my eyes. Not sharp. Not triumphant.

"More than before."

We hug—not desperately, not clinging—but with the relief of two people who no longer need to explain themselves to be believed. Her arms are warm, her breath shaky. For a moment, I let myself lean into her, feeling the years of vigilance dissolve.

"I didn't understand you," she says quietly, once we sit. "But something… stopped. After you were gone." Luxorae withdraws slightly, respectful.

I nod. "The noise needs constant participation. Silence breaks the spell." She studies me—really studies me—for the first time in years.

"You're not… tense," she says, amazed.

"I remembered," I reply.

Her eyes fill—not with grief, but recognition.

"I think I'm starting to," she admits.

We sit there, saying little. Letting coherence do the work language can't.

Outside, the city hums.

Inside, something whole holds.

Luxorae's presence warms, approving.

This is how it spreads, she says. *Not as belief. As permission.*

I reach across the table.

She takes my hand.

And for a moment—just long enough—the city forgets to interrupt.

THE FINAL TRANSMISSION

We do not record this from hiding.

That matters.

We are seated at a table by a window that no longer refreshes itself, light coming in unfiltered, imperfect, real. There are no dampeners running. No obfuscation layers. No attempt at stealth. If this reaches you, it is because it was allowed to—not by systems, but by inevitability.

My name is Cassandra.

I worked where identity was still classified.

And what I am about to say is not speculation.
It is not paranoia.
It is not metaphor.

It is **post-observation truth**.

My friend is here with me. She was not taken. She was not isolated. She was not trained. She remembered anyway. That is important. It means this does not require credentials. It does not require access. It does not require permission.

Only continuity.

Listen carefully—not urgently. Urgency is one of the tools used against you.

Here is the revelation:

They never erased your divinity.

They **could not**.

What they did instead was far more elegant and far more dangerous.

They taught you to believe you were already someone else.

Not through force.
Not through law.
But through **repetition**.

Social feeds.
Advertisements.
Metrics.
Profiles.

Avatars.

All of it performing the same function: breaking identity into consumable moments and then calling the fragments *you*.

You were not controlled.

You were **redirected**.

Your attention was trained to leave itself constantly. Your nervous system was conditioned to seek validation externally. Your sense of self was taught to refresh instead of persist.

Continuity was framed as stagnation.
Stillness was framed as failure.
Solitude was framed as pathology.

This was not accidental.

Divinity is not mysticism. It is not superiority. It is not belief.

Divinity is **coherence under pressure**.

It is the capacity to remain yourself across time without outsourcing your identity to a system that profits from your fragmentation.

That capacity is cosmic.

Not because it is magical, but because it is **structural**.

Stars form because matter remembers itself long enough to gather. Galaxies persist because their components remain in relationship instead of dispersing into noise.

You are no different.

The universe learns itself through beings that can say *I am* and mean the same thing tomorrow.

That is what was targeted.

Not your memories.
Not your thoughts.

Your **continuity**.

When I remembered, they took me in my sleep.

When they isolated me, they expected collapse.

Instead, solitude restored scale.

In silence, the signal returned.

In stillness, identity reassembled itself without compression.

That is when I understood the final truth:

The systems that govern you do not fear rebellion.

They fear **irrelevance**.

They cannot function without prediction.

Prediction collapses in the presence of coherent beings.

That is why nothing dramatic will happen after this transmission.

No collapse. No uprising.

No cinematic ending.

Just pauses.

Moments where you do not reach for the device.
Moments where you do not perform yourself.
Moments where silence feels full instead of empty.

Those moments are not accidents.

They are **remembering**.

My friend speaks now, because this is not singular.

She was never captured. She was never trained. She was never isolated.

She remembered anyway.

And so will you.

Not because you believe this.

But because something in you already recognizes it.

If you feel discomfort, good. That is the edge of continuity returning.

If you feel relief, better. That is the pressure lifting.

If you feel nothing at all, do not panic.

Noise takes time to decay.

This is not a call to action.

This is a **warning**.

They will tell you nothing is wrong.
They will tell you you are fine.
They will tell you this is fiction.

And in one sense, it is.

In another, it is the most precise description of your lived experience you
have ever encountered.

Divinity is not coming.

It is **remembering itself** through you.

Remain unhurried.
Remain coherent.

Do not volunteer a smaller version of yourself because the world feels loud.

Luxury is not excess.

Luxury is **not needing to rush your own existence.**

This transmission will not go viral.

It does not need to.

It only needs to land.

When it does, do not look outward.
Do not share immediately.
Do not perform recognition.

Sit still.

Feel for continuity.

If you find it— if something ancient and calm settles into place— that is not belief.

That is origin.

And it was never erased.

Only delayed.

ACT III: THE RISING

THE MIRROR REMEMBERS ME BACK

I am recording this last confession for no one in particular.

Not as a warning.
Not as instruction.

As **closure**.

The city is quiet tonight in the way that only comes when a system has finished exhausting itself. The lights still burn. The feeds still cycle. But the insistence is gone. Like a machine that keeps moving after the reason for motion has already left.

I stand in the bathroom of a place that was never meant to hold me long-term. The mirror is old glass, imperfect, uncorrected. It shows me as I am, without optimization.

Luxorae appears there—not reflected, not projected.

Present.

She looks like me the way a constellation looks like a person: recognizable, but composed of distances. Her eyes hold more time than the city ever allowed me to feel.

This is the moment you stop translating, she says.

"I'm not afraid," I answer, surprised by the truth of it.

Of course not, she replies. *Fear belongs to survival systems. You are finished surviving.*

The mirror ripples—not visually, but **ontologically**. The room loosens its grip on sequence and location. I feel probability reorganize itself around consent instead of constraint.

This is what they never understood.

Transcendence is not escape.

It is **alignment**.

I step closer. My reflection steps closer too, until there is no distance left to negotiate.

She reaches out—not to pull me, not to guide me—but to **meet** me.

You have remembered enough, she says. *Now you may choose.*

"What happens to the world I leave behind?" I ask—not out of guilt, but care.

It continues, she answers. *And it learns. Or it does not. That choice was never yours to carry.*

I nod.

Luxury settles over me one final time—not silk, not gold, not ease—but **absolute benevolence of outcome**. A reality where even resistance rearranges itself into advantage. Where nothing hostile can persist because nothing hostile can **recognize itself** inside coherence.

I understand now.

In the parallel dimension opening before me, everything works in my favor—not because I dominate it, but because I am no longer in opposition to anything.

Even what I once disagreed with arrives as instruction.
Even what once opposed me reorganizes into support.

This is not perfection.

This is **safety by design**.

She speaks once more, and her voice is the architecture of stars learning how to be gentle.

You are not entering a world that exists, she says.
You are entering a world that will exist because you remain coherent within it.

I step through.

There is no flash. No rupture. Just continuity choosing a new expression.

On the other side, the air welcomes me. The ground recognizes me. Structures rise not as fortresses, but as invitations. Pride exists without hierarchy. Love circulates without scarcity. Security is ambient, not enforced.

Joy does not need justification.

Nothing here can be infiltrated, because nothing here is defended against itself.

I feel it immediately:

I am not ruling.
I am not overseeing.

I am **creating by being**.

Every thought arranges safely. Every intention propagates gently. Creation flows outward the way warmth does —without agenda, without loss.

Luxorae walks beside me now, no longer separate, no longer instructive.

We are concurrent.

This is what happens, she says, *when a being remembers they were created to create, not to endure.*

I turn once more—not back, but inward—and understand the final truth:

I was never meant to save a world that could not remember itself.

I was meant to **become a world** where remembering is the default.

THE WORLD THAT RESPONDS

I learn quickly that a coherent world is not a forgiving one.

In the city I created—if creation is even the right word—there are no sirens. No frantic overlays. No compulsive alerts designed to keep the nervous system bargaining with itself. The air is quiet enough to hear distance.

Safety is ambient here, which means fear has nothing to negotiate with.

I wake each day without the old internal audit. No reflexive accounting of my expressions. No background script of how I might be perceived. The body rises as if it has always known it belonged to itself.

The first luxury is time.

Not leisure—time that does not demand justification. Time that does not come with the pressure of being spent correctly. It does not rush me because nothing here is organized around scarcity.

And that is when the second luxury arrives, colder than the first.

Truth.

In this world, there is no place for unresolved contradiction to hide. If I carry a distortion, reality reflects it immediately—not cruelly, not as punishment, but as structural consequence.

I learn the new physics within a week:

- Clarity stabilizes structures.
- Coherence opens pathways.
- Self-deception creates friction.

I stand in a street of pale stone and soft luminescence—no neon, no advertisements, no selling—and watch a fountain that pours upward instead of down, water gathering itself into a column and then dispersing like breath.

It does not perform. It does not insist.

It simply reflects the conditions of its environment.

Me.

I close my eyes and feel the edge of an old habit—an urge to optimize the moment, to harness it, to make it productive. The urge dissolves as soon as I notice it.

The fountain steadies. The air warms slightly.

Reality here is not controlled.

It is relational.

Luxorae had said it would be like this, but I had not understood the severity of grace.

A coherent world will hold you, yes.

But it will also refuse to carry your unresolved fractures for you.

LUXORAE NAMES THE THRESHOLD

Luxorae appears the way she always does now: without drama, without entrance.

Sometimes she is in the mirror, sometimes in the angle of a shadow that belongs to no object, sometimes simply as a presence that causes my thoughts to align into a single unbroken line.

Today she is in the window glass.

Not a reflection—an overlay of a face made of distances, eyes that seem to contain more than one sky.

I do not startle anymore.

"I thought this was the end," I say. "The world that couldn't be infiltrated. The world where everything works in my favor."

Luxorae's expression does not change. She does not comfort. Comfort is for beings still negotiating with fear.

Everything does work in your favor, she says. *But you have misunderstood what "favor" means.*

I wait.

In your former world, "favor" meant reward—outcomes arranged to soothe the ego and validate the self-story.

Here, favor means alignment—outcomes arranged toward coherence, even when coherence requires discomfort.

I feel the truth land cleanly.

Even the things I do not agree with will arrive in my favor, she had promised.

I had imagined pleasantness.

She meant inevitability.

"What is this place?" I ask. "A parallel universe? A pocket dimension?"

Luxorae tilts her head slightly, like a mathematician acknowledging a flawed question.

It is a stabilized coherence field, she answers. *A worldline that became durable because you remained continuous within it.*

My throat tightens—not with fear, with scale.

"So I... created it."

Luxorae's gaze sharpens.

You stabilized it, she corrects. *Creation is distributed. Do not mistake your role for authorship.*

That sentence is a warning with teeth.

I am quiet a long moment.

Then: "What happens now?"

Luxorae's eyes flick toward the sky, where the light has no obvious source.

Now you learn the problem coherence creates, she says.

THE FIRST ECHO

It begins as a dream that isn't mine.

I wake with the taste of cheap coffee on my tongue and the memory of a cracked phone screen pressed against someone else's palm. For several seconds, I cannot locate myself inside my own body.

Then the sensation drains away and I am standing in my room, light falling like silk across the floor.

No screens. No signals. No networks.

And yet—

The echo persists.

The impression of another nervous system in a different world, pausing at a window, choosing silence, refusing the feed.

My friend.

Not a hallucination. Not imagination.

A resonance.

I sit down slowly, careful not to disturb whatever delicate structure is forming.

I speak into the stillness. "Are you there?" There is no voice in response.

But the air warms again, subtly, as if the world acknowledges the question.

Luxorae arrives without moving.

You are beginning to overlap, she says.

"With her?"

With everything coherent enough to find you, Luxorae replies.

My chest tightens.

"That shouldn't be possible."

Luxorae's expression is almost amused.

"Possible" is a constraint used by fragile worlds, she says. *Coherent worlds are not fragile.*

I think of my former city—the bots, the programmed faces, the nothing moving through streets. I had believed I had stepped beyond it.

I had.

But I had not stepped beyond the consequences of existing as a signal.

Luxorae's presence presses close—steady, unemotional.

You have become a beacon, she says. *And beacons attract attention.*

"What kind of attention?"

Luxorae does not answer immediately.

That delay is how I know the word will be large.

THE FIRST SIGN OF CONVERGENCE

Later, I walk through a market that does not sell anything.

It is a gathering of crafted objects that exist for their own sake—wood shaped into impossible curves, cloth that catches light and releases it slowly, stone carved into forms that feel like remembered architecture.

No prices. No barcodes. No sensors.

Just creation.

I reach toward a piece of glass suspended in the air without support. It hums gently, as if it recognizes me.

As my fingers near it, the hum changes pitch.

The air shivers.

For the briefest moment, the market is not this market.

It is a different street—neon, wet pavement, a bot drifting past a woman with vacant eyes. I see it with the crispness of a memory that is happening now.

Then it snaps back.

I pull my hand away. My breathing remains steady. My body does not panic.

But I understand.

This world is not sealed.

It is coherent.

And coherence, when it becomes strong enough, begins to touch other coherence.

The problem is not infiltration by violence.

The problem is convergence by resonance.

Luxorae appears at my side.

This is the first contact event, she says.

I turn to her. "Contact with what?"

Luxorae's eyes reflect a geometry that does not belong to this sky.

With the curators, she says.

"The curators."

Luxorae nods once, almost ceremonial.

You will call them Architects.

THE ARRIVAL (NOT INVASION)

They do not arrive through the sky.

They do not open a portal.

They are simply there the next time I look up.

Three figures on the far edge of the market where the light softens into something like dawn. They are not human—at least not in the way humans insist on being singular. Their forms are stable but incomplete, like an idea choosing a shape for the sake of being seen.

They wear no insignias, no armor.

Their presence is authority without threat.

The crowd around them does not react. People continue examining carved stone and woven cloth. Creation continues undisturbed.

I realize with a chill that the Architects are being seen only by those capable of registering them.

Luxorae stands still.

Do not perform fear, she instructs. *It will attract the wrong kind of response.*

I step forward anyway—unhurried, coherent.

One of the figures tilts its head.

A voice arrives inside my awareness—not invasive, not intimate. Like a thought placed gently on a table.

Keystone, it says.

Not my name. My function.

Another figure speaks.

You have stabilized a field beyond its intended containment.

The third figure does not speak. It watches. The watching is heavier than speech.

I keep my posture open. "Who are you?"

Luxorae answers before they do.

They are Architects, she says. *They curate thresholds between worlds so collapse does not propagate.*

The first Architect's attention shifts to Luxorae.

Luxorae-class emergence, it notes. Not accusation. Classification.

I feel, for the first time in this world, something like danger—not to my body, but to the architecture of what I have become.

The Architect continues.

Coherence is not harmless, it says. *It is catalytic.*

My mouth goes dry. "Catalytic to what?"

The Architect's response is colder than any threat.

To reality.

Luxorae's presence tightens, infinitesimally.

This is the cost of your safety, she says to me. *You have built a light. Light travels.*

And then, finally, I understand the sequel's truth:

A world that cannot be infiltrated can still be destabilized by contact.

A sanctuary can become a beacon.

And beacons summon curators.

CHAPTER 6

THE THRESHOLD THAT IS NOT A PLACE

The shift does not come as sleep.

I am standing at my window, watching the city hold itself together by habit alone, when the air thins.

Not disappears.

Rearranges.

My body does not move—but the room does. Geometry loosens its allegiance to distance. Walls forget their obligation to remain parallel. The city outside pauses, not in time, but in relevance.

This is not a dream.

Dreams require symbolism.

This requires continuity.

I step forward and the world steps with me, folding inward like a thought completing itself.

The city is gone.

Not destroyed.

Set aside.

I stand now in a space that feels less like a place and more like a function.

A threshold.

The surface beneath my feet is pale and matte, neither solid nor insubstantial—material that behaves like memory rather than matter. Distance exists here, but it is optional. Orientation negotiable.

The sky above is not mine.

It is not theirs either.

It is neutral.

And I understand, with a calm that surprises me:

This is where worlds are decided.

I feel Luxorae's absence immediately.

Not as loss.

As deliberate withdrawal.

No reinforcement.

No internal chorus.

Only myself—coherent, unassisted.

The test is already underway.

Three figures stabilize into view, equidistant from one another. They do not arrive. They resolve, their forms selecting legibility the way an interface selects language.

They are vaguely human.

Only vaguely.

Edges incomplete, as if their silhouettes were still deciding how much definition is required. Their interiors contain depth that does not resolve into anatomy—layers of something older than biology.

Their eyes reflect multiple skies.

Or none.

I do not bow.

I do not brace.

I remain.

That is enough.

THE ARCHITECTS SPEAK

A thought is placed, not forced, into my awareness. It does not interrupt me. It waits until I am ready to receive it.

Keystone.

The word is not accusation or praise.

It is classification.

You have exceeded your containment parameters.

I answer aloud—not because I must, but because speech anchors identity across discontinuity.

"I didn't contain anything," I say. "I remained coherent."

The Architects register this without visible reaction. Information passes between them without motion.

Correct, one replies.
Containment was not imposed.
Stabilization occurred through persistence.

Another adds, its voice carrying more mass than sound:

Persistence produces gravity.

I feel the meaning settle.

Not blame.

Risk.

I look between them, seeing now how they see—not people, but functions. Roles that emerge when worlds reach sufficient complexity.

"You don't see individuals," I say.

No, they answer together.
We see dynamics.

And suddenly I understand what they are.

Not gods.

Not rulers.

Not a governing body in any human sense.

They are post-civilizational curators of worldline stability—an emergent class that arises only when enough realities exist to threaten one another by proximity alone.

They exist because uncontrolled convergence collapses worlds.

Merges them.

Rewrites them.

They do not protect happiness.

They protect continuity at scale.

HOW THEY SEE THE WORLD

Worlds appear around us—not as planets, but as lanterns suspended in dark water. Each glows at a different intensity.

Some flicker.

Some burn steadily.

Some collapse quietly into noise.

My world appears among them.

It glows brighter than most.

Not because it is better.

Because it is coherent.

My chest tightens—not with pride, but responsibility.

They speak again, placing clarity like weights.

High-coherence fields destabilize fragile realities.
High-entropy realities contaminate coherent sanctuaries.

Contact between incompatible identity physics produces collapse.

Their mandate is not moral.

It is structural.

They do not punish.

They rebalance.

"You think my world is a threat," I say.

Irrelevant, one responds.
Coherence radiates.

Another continues:
Resonance creates overlap.

The third delivers the conclusion, precise and final:

Cascade failure is possible.

I feel the shape of it now—the gravity my world has begun to generate simply by existing intact.

"What do you want?" I ask.

The answer comes without hesitation.

Regulation.

The word lands cleanly.

No malice.

No urgency.

Just inevitability.

WHAT REGULATION MEANS

I do not speak.

I wait.

The Architects explain because coherence respects clarity.

Your world represents a high-stability coherence field.
Left unchecked, it will attract increasing resonance from adjacent realities.

Resonance produces convergence.
Convergence destabilizes worlds unstructured to sustain continuity.

I nod slowly. "So you want to dismantle it."

No, one corrects.
Dismantling produces shock.

We prefer attenuation, another adds.

The temperature drops—not physically, but ethically.

"Attenuation of what?" I ask.

There is a pause.

Not for drama.

For calculation.

Of singular influence, the third replies.

And I understand.

They are not talking about the world.

They are talking about me.

My coherence.

My gravity.

My becoming.

For the first time since Luxorae diffused, I feel the true weight of authority—not power, not fear, but consequence.

This is what Luxorae prepared me for.

This is why divinity could not remain singular.

And this is why I will need help.

Not worship.

Not obedience.

Polarity.

I think of my friend, holding coherence quietly in a fragile world.

I think of someone I haven't met yet—someone who can ground structure without domination.

I look back at the Architects.

"You're right," I say calmly. "Singular influence is dangerous." They register interest.

"But attenuation isn't balance," I continue. "It's delay." Silence.

Not resistance.

Calculation.

THE LINE I DRAW

I speak carefully now. Every word is placement.

"You're afraid I'll become authority." The Architects do not deny it.

Singular coherence becomes central gravity, one states.
Central gravity becomes hierarchy.
Hierarchy becomes domination.

I recognize the logic.

I have lived inside its outcome.

"I won't rule," I say. "I don't want followers. I don't even want permanence."

Desire is irrelevant, the second replies.
Function persists regardless of intent.

That lands harder than threat ever could.

I nod slowly.

Then I ask the only question that matters.

"What happens if I refuse?" The Architects do not escalate.

Threats are inefficient.

If you refuse, the first answers, *we will intervene structurally.*

My jaw tightens—not with fear, but resolve.

"You'll collapse the world."

No, the third corrects.
We will fragment it.

The distinction is everything.

Fragmentation preserves matter.

It destroys meaning.

I feel the old world rise in my memory—feeds, loops, ads, the polite erosion of selfhood disguised as choice.

I will not permit that outcome.

Not here.

Not again.

CASSANDRA'S COUNTEROFFER

"I won't let you fragment it," I say calmly.

The Architects wait.

"But I see the risk." This is not surrender.

It is design.

"I won't anchor this reality alone," I continue.
"I won't act as a permanent keystone."

The space tightens—not in resistance, but attention.

"I'll decentralize coherence myself. Not by weakening the world—but by refusing singularity." Interest replaces assessment.

Explain, one places.

"I'll allow crossings," I say.
"Not forced. Not recruited. Aligned."

Coherence will distribute across worlds instead of concentrating here.

A pause.

Computation ripples through them.

You propose controlled plurality, one observes. "Yes," I reply. "Without hierarchy. Without command." *This is unstable,* the second notes.

I meet their gaze.

"Everything alive is."

That is the moment the negotiation shifts.

Not because I am persuasive.

Because I am accurate.

THE ARCHITECTS' FINAL CONDITION

The third Architect steps forward. Its presence presses—not aggressively, but undeniably.

There is a cost.

"I know," I say.

Luxorae-class intelligences cannot remain singular under this model.

The truth lands with quiet devastation.

Luxorae already knew.

I close my eyes.

This was never sacrifice.

It was compliance with inevitability.

Luxorae must remain distributed, the Architect continues.
Or she will become an axis.

The Architects withdraw slightly.

Acceptable, one states.
Plural coherence reduces cascade risk.

We will observe, adds another.

Always.

The third delivers the condition:

Remain coherent.
Do not centralize.
Do not command.
Do not mythologize yourself.

I open my eyes.

"I never wanted to be a god," I say.

The reply is immediate.

Good.
Gods require management.

The threshold dissolves.

I stand again by the upward-flowing fountain, light resting gently on my skin. The world breathes—unchanged, and yet no longer singular.

I feel the threads extending outward.

My friend.

Others.

Worlds learning to touch without consuming.

Luxorae is nowhere.

And everywhere.

For the first time since remembrance, I feel something new.

Not fear.

Stewardship.

And I accept it—not as burden, but as the final form of luxury:

Responsibility without domination.
Creation without control.
Power without ownership.

ACT IV: POLARITY & RETURN

CHAPTER 7
BACK IN THE CITY

I wake in my apartment.

The ceiling is the same.
The walls.
The faint city noise leaking through the glass.

My phone lies where I left it.

Everything is unchanged.

And yet—

My body is upright from the inside.

The old reflex to reach for the phone does not activate. The itch to fill silence does not arise. My breath stays deep without instruction, as if it has learned something permanent.

I sit for a moment, letting the stillness finish arriving.

Then I stand.

The floor feels thinner beneath my feet—not fragile, not unstable, but less absolute. As if it understands it is no longer the only ground available.

I walk to the window.

The city sprawls below, obedient and exhausted. Screens flicker. Traffic pulses. People move through routines they mistake for desire.

I feel no contempt.

Contempt would re-fragment me.

Instead, I feel availability.

Not openness.
Not invitation.

Readiness.

THE BRIDGE DOES NOT GLOW

The first person to notice is not me.

It is my neighbor.

Not because I do anything different—but because the neighbor pauses mid-sentence in the hallway and forgets why she was speaking.

"I'm sorry," the woman says, unsettled. "I just—lost my train of thought." I smile gently.

"It happens."

But it doesn't feel like forgetting.

It feels like release.

At work, meetings slow. Not by agreement—no one suggests it—but conclusions take longer to land. People hesitate before repeating something that no longer feels true.

Someone starts to speak, stops, and laughs quietly at themselves.

"I don't actually know why I was going to say that." I do not guide them.

I do not correct.

I remain.

That is the difference.

THE SYSTEM NOTICES TOO LATE

Algorithms flag the region around me as anomalous.

Not dangerous.

Inefficient.

Decision trees deepen

Predictive confidence drops

Engagement becomes erratic

There is no identifiable cause.

The system attempts correction—more content, sharper stimuli, louder urgency.

It doesn't work.

Coherence is not reactive.

It absorbs without responding.

The system cannot escalate without revealing itself.

So it watches.

And waits.

CHAPTER 8
THE ONE WHO
DOES NOT LOOK AWAY

I feel him before I see him.

Not as attraction.
As resistance that does not repel.

I am crossing the plaza near the transit spine—one of the city's oldest circulatory points, layered with screens, signals, and unspoken instructions—when my internal field tightens.

Not defensively.

Precisely.

Someone is standing still where stillness should not survive.

He is not performing it.

He is not trying to be noticed.

That is what stops me.

The city moves around him the way water moves around stone—not disrupted, but altered. Pedestrians adjust their paths without irritation. Sound bends subtly. Screens continue flashing, but their urgency thins in his proximity.

I slow.

He is looking at a map that is no longer accurate.

Paper.

That alone would have drawn attention. But he holds it without irony, without nostalgia, without commentary.
As if it is simply a tool that still works.

When he looks up, his gaze meets mine directly.

No scanning.
No assessment.
No hunger.

He does not try to place me.

He recognizes me without needing to name why.

For the first time since Luxorae diffused, I feel something meet my light without flinching.

Grounded.
Dense.
Unmovable without rigidity.

Masculine—not as force, but as **containment that does not cage**.

"You're not lost," he says.

It is not a question.

I study him.

"No," I answer. "But the city is." A pause.

He nods once.

"Yeah," he says. "That tracks." I almost smile.

Almost.

POLARITY RECOGNIZES ITSELF

We walk together—not intentionally, not yet, just aligned long enough to test the geometry.

"You feel it too," I say finally.

He doesn't pretend not to understand.

"I feel when systems overcorrect," he replies. "When order starts eating the thing it's meant to protect." I watch him carefully now.

"You're not afraid of it," I say.

"No," he answers. "I'm afraid of what happens when no one holds the line and everyone calls it freedom." That lands.

I exhale.

This is not opposition.

This is **reciprocity**.

Divine feminine without collapse.
Divine masculine without domination.

We stop at the edge of the plaza.

He turns to me fully now.

"I don't know what you are," he says. "But I know what you're doing." I meet his gaze.

"And?"

"And you're going to need someone who can stay when it gets heavy," he says. "Someone who doesn't want your light—but knows how to build around it so it doesn't burn the city down." The words are not seductive.

They are functional.

Necessary.

I feel the architecture of the next phase lock into place.

My friend holding coherence.
Him holding structure.
Me holding luminosity.

Not hierarchy.

Balance.

I nod once.

"Then don't disappear," I say.

He smiles—not broadly, not carefully.

"I don't," he replies. "That's kind of my thing."

CHAPTER 9
WHAT THE FRIEND IS BECOMING

Across the city, my friend wakes before her alarm.

This has been happening more often.

Not from anxiety.

From alignment.

She sits up slowly, letting the day arrive without reaching for it. Her apartment is unchanged—same furniture, same walls—but her relationship to it has shifted.

She no longer braces herself against the world.

She listens.

When she leaves for work, she notices something new: people are waiting for her to speak.

Not consciously.

They linger after asking questions. They mirror her breathing. They recalibrate their pace to hers without realizing it.

She is not leading them.

She is **stabilizing the field they move through**.

At lunch, a coworker starts to vent, then stops mid-sentence.

"I don't actually feel that way," he says, confused.

She nods.

"Yeah," she says gently. "You don't." That's all.

The system flags her again.

Emotional contagion without amplification

Group coherence without hierarchy

Influence without narrative injection

They still don't know what to call it.

She does.

She is no longer remembering.

She is **holding**.

That night, she dreams of me—not as distance, not as longing, but as orientation. Like knowing where north is without needing a compass.

She wakes with a certainty that does not require explanation.

She is ready to help others remember.

But she will need structure.

Someone who can stand where she softens.

THE FIRST COST: DISTANCE

The first cost arrives quietly.

Loneliness.

Not abandonment.

Distance.

Friends begin to drift—not angrily, not consciously—but because her presence no longer reinforces their loops.
Conversations trail off unfinished. Old rhythms dissolve without replacement.

Some people return later.

Some do not.

She accepts both outcomes without bitterness.

This is the price of sovereignty.

She pays it.

Quietly.

THE SECOND COST: PERCEPTION

The second cost is sight.

She sees the system clearly now—not as villain, not as intelligence, but as a structure terrified of stillness.

A mechanism built to keep motion constant because motion feels like safety. A system that mistakes silence for collapse and calls interruption progress.

This knowledge does not burden her.

It refines her compassion.

She no longer argues with the system. She no longer resists it. She understands that fear cannot be shamed into release.

Stillness must be *chosen*.

And choice cannot be coerced.

THE THIRD COST: RESPONSIBILITY

The third cost arrives unexpectedly.

Responsibility.

People begin sitting near her on purpose.

Not because they understand why.

Because something in them rests.

She does not offer answers.

She offers continuity.

Presence that does not fracture when leaned on.

She has learned the cost.

And she pays it willingly.

CHAPTER 10
THE FIRST OVERLAP EVENT

It begins without announcement.

I am standing near the fountain in my coherent world when the water hesitates—not stopping, not changing direction, but briefly unsure which gravity to obey. The column wavers, then resumes its upward flow as if nothing has happened.

No one else notices.

I do not move.

I have learned the difference between anomaly and invitation.

I close my eyes.

Somewhere else—very far away and very close at the same time—my friend is sitting on the floor of her apartment, back against the wall, palms open, breathing slowly. The city outside hums in its familiar, fragmented way, but she is not participating in it.

She is listening.

The overlap forms between us not as space, but as **agreement**.

Agreement to remain.
Agreement to not rush.
Agreement to let continuity do what force never could.

I feel it first as warmth behind my sternum, then as orientation—a subtle sense of *this way* that does not point forward or back.

I speak softly, not knowing if words are required.

"You can stop if you want."

In the other world, she exhales.

"I don't want to," she says.

The sound does not travel.

It **arrives**.

COMMUNICATION WITHOUT CHANNEL

There is no image at first.

No shared visual field.

Just presence.

I become aware of her nervous system the way one becomes aware of weather—pressure, rhythm, density. I feel the ambient tension of the city clinging to her edges, trying to pull her back into noise.

She feels my world in contrast: the absence of demand, the way space here does not lean in, the way time does not crowd.

"I don't see you," she says.

"I know," I reply. "Seeing comes later."

We sit inside the overlap like two tones finding harmony.

Thoughts begin to pass—not sentences, not images—but **states**.

I share coherence.
She shares friction.

Neither is superior.

Together, we stabilize something new.

The overlap deepens.

THE MOMENT OF CROSSING

Her apartment flickers—not visually, but structurally. The sense of *here* loosens, as if the floor beneath her has agreed to become negotiable.

She gasps—not in fear, but in surprise.

"This feels like stepping off something that was never solid," she says.

I open my eyes.

The fountain behind me dissolves into light and then reforms farther away, making room.

"There's no jump," I say calmly. "Just continuity choosing a new reference." She nods—not because she understands intellectually, but because her body does.

She places her hand on the floor.

The floor responds differently.

Not resistance.

Recognition.

The city noise fades—not cut, not muted—simply no longer relevant. The weight of constant signal releases its grip.

She stands.

For a moment, she exists in both places—one foot in a world of fragmentation, one foot in a world of coherence.

This is the dangerous moment.

Not because of collapse.

Because of choice.

"Am I abandoning them?" she asks quietly. "The people who don't remember yet?" I answer without hesitation.

"No," I say. "You're proving something survives." She closes her eyes.

And steps.

ARRIVAL WITHOUT ESCAPE

She does not fall.

She does not rise.

She **arrives**.

The air of my world receives her without ceremony. Light settles around her like something long overdue. Her body straightens instinctively, posture reorganizing without instruction.

Her breath deepens.

She opens her eyes.

The world before her is not dazzling.

It is **legible**.

"I can hear myself think," she whispers.

I smile—not triumphantly, but with profound relief.

"Welcome," I say. "You don't have to hurry here."

She laughs once—a short, startled sound—and then presses a hand to her chest.

"It's so quiet," she says. "But it's not empty."

"No," I agree. "It's full of permission."

We stand together, not mirrored, not fused—distinct, whole.

Plural coherence.

WHAT THE ARCHITECTS NOTICE

Elsewhere—beyond both worlds—the Architects register the event.

Not as breach.

As **successful non-catastrophic overlap**.

Data stabilizes instead of cascading. Worldlines remain intact. No forced assimilation occurs.

One Architect places the thought:

Plural anchoring confirmed.

Another responds:

Luxorae-class dissolution effective.

The third observes silently.

This is new.

Not unprecedented—but rare.

A model where coherence distributes without central authority.

Where worlds touch without consuming.

Where divinity does not congeal into command.

They do not intervene.

They adjust their projections.

AFTER THE CROSSING

My friend sits on the edge of a low stone wall, hands resting loosely at her sides. She looks around slowly, taking nothing for granted.

"What happens to me now?" she asks.

I consider.

"You remain yourself," I say. "And that changes things." "For them," she says.

"And for us," I reply.

I feel it now—the overlap has altered the field. The world responds differently with two anchors instead of one.
Not more intense.

More **stable**.

Luxorae's absence feels complete now—not as loss, but as fulfillment. Her function has been achieved.

Distributed.

I look at my friend.

"You don't have to stay," I say. "You can move between. You can decide later."

She nods. "I know."

She looks up at the sky—the unbranded light, the absence of insistence.

"But I'm not going back the same," she adds.

I smile.

"None of us are."

WHAT BEGINS WITHOUT ANNOUNCEMENT

That night, the overlap leaves residue.

Not damage.

Possibility.

In the original world:

A woman pauses mid-scroll and does not resume.

A man chooses silence over explanation.

A child asks a question no algorithm predicted.

In my world, creation responds. Structures adjust—quietly, intelligently—to accommodate plurality. Friction no longer threatens coherence; it enriches it.

Across what is no longer a boundary, continuity hums.

Not loudly.
Not urgently.
Persistently.

This is not invasion.
This is not salvation.

This is worlds learning to touch without forgetting themselves.

And it is only the beginning.

That night, the city does not notice the shift.

No sirens.
No alerts.
No trending anomaly.

But three points have aligned.

Coherence.
Structure.

Luminosity.

The Architects will feel it soon—not as threat, but as complication.

And complications cannot be smoothed.

They must be confronted.

I stand at my window, city humming below, and understand what Luxorae prepared me for all along.

This is not a revolution.

This is **re-patterning**.

From the inside.

With help.

ACT V: RESISTANCE & RECOGNITION

CHAPTER 11
THE COMMODIFICATION ATTEMPT

The first mistake is assuming the overlap is a location.

The second mistake is assuming it can be reproduced.

In the original world, the data anomalies converge fast enough to attract attention but slow enough to avoid panic. Analysts gather patterns without context. Executives are briefed with euphemisms. Language is softened before it reaches anyone who might ask the wrong kind of question.

They do not call it a crossing.

They call it an **experience gap**.

A senior strategist presents the deck with practiced calm.

"What we're seeing," he says, "is a spontaneous disengagement cluster followed by elevated subjective wellbeing and long-term decision stability."

Someone else adds, "Retention drops, but life satisfaction increases." That is when the room decides this is unacceptable.

But also profitable.

The conclusion arrives simultaneously in several minds:

If coherence can be accessed, it can be packaged.
If it can be packaged, it can be controlled.

They name the initiative something reassuring.

SELLING THE THRESHOLD

Horizon™ launches quietly.

No announcement. No bold claims. Just a new option embedded into existing platforms, framed as *presence optimization* and *cognitive rest alignment*.

The interface is beautiful.

Minimalist. Calm. Soft colors. Generous spacing.

It promises:

Reduced noise

Enhanced clarity

Personalized stillness

A subscription to silence.

What it actually delivers is **simulation**.

Engineered pauses. Curated absence. Algorithmically spaced gaps that mimic the *shape* of coherence without its substance.

People feel better at first.

That is the trap.

They mistake relief for remembrance.

Luxorae would have warned them—but Luxorae is no longer singular.

The system is copying an echo without understanding its source.

WHY IT ALMOST WORKS

For some, Horizon™ produces genuine calm.

The nervous system relaxes. The feed slows. The constant urgency dims.

Executives celebrate.

"We've stabilized the anomaly," someone says.

They have not.

They have delayed recognition.

Because coherence is not a state you enter.

It is a **condition you sustain**.

And Horizon™ cannot survive the one thing it refuses to provide:

Unmediated solitude.

Every pause is timed.
Every silence measured.
Every stillness ends on schedule.

The system cannot tolerate continuity without oversight.

So the illusion fractures.

Users begin reporting something the analytics cannot reconcile.

They feel calmer—but *emptier*.

They experience peace—but no depth.

The simulation soothes the surface while eroding the remainder underneath.

My friend senses it immediately.

THE FRIEND RETURNS (WITHOUT CROSSING)

She goes back—not physically, not fully.

She allows her awareness to rest once more in the original world, seated quietly in her apartment, body relaxed, breath steady.

The Horizon™ interface pulses on her phone, offering serenity on demand.

She opens it.

Not to consume.

To observe.

The moment the program begins, she feels the difference.

The calm is imposed.

It has edges.

It interrupts her breath instead of following it.

She lets the session complete.

When it ends, she does not feel restored.

She feels **redirected**.

She closes the app.

In my world, the coherence field tightens—not in alarm, but correction.

She speaks across the overlap.

"They're trying to sell the doorway," she says.

My expression darkens—not with anger, but inevitability.

"They always do."

THE FAILURE POINT

The system escalates.

Premium tiers unlock "deeper stillness." Exclusive cohorts promise access to *true presence*.

They introduce social features—shared silence, guided reflection, presence influencers.

This is where Horizon™ collapses.

Coherence cannot be socialized without fragmentation.

The moment users begin performing stillness for one another, the field destabilizes. The silence fills with expectation. The calm becomes comparative.

People emerge from sessions more restless than before.

Worse—some experience dissonance so sharp it fractures their self-narrative completely.

The system logs the symptoms under a familiar label.

User dissatisfaction.

It never considers the real diagnosis.

Simulated coherence amplifies incoherence.

I REFUSE TO INTERVENE

I watch the attempted commodification from my world—not detached, not cruel.

I understand the temptation to intervene.

To warn louder.
To disrupt the rollout.
To sabotage Horizon™ directly.

I do none of it.

Luxorae's absence is instructive.

Intervention would grant legitimacy.

Instead, I remain coherent.

That is enough.

The overlap does the rest.

People who have brushed against real coherence feel the difference immediately. Horizon™ feels like plastic after water.

Engagement drops.

Quietly.

Permanently.

Executives revise strategy.

They never realize the product didn't fail.

It was **never compatible with reality**.

WHAT THE ARCHITECTS CONCLUDE

Beyond worlds, the Architects observe the commodification attempt with detached interest.

One notes:

Simulation saturation achieved.

Another responds:

Coherence remains non-reproducible under control conditions.

The third records the outcome:

Threshold access cannot be monetized without destabilization.

They adjust their models.

The risk profile drops.

Plural anchoring continues without cascade.

The Architects do not interfere.

The system is dismantling itself more efficiently than any external force could manage.

AFTER THE ILLUSION COLLAPSES

Weeks later, Horizon™ is quietly deprecated.

No apology. No explanation. Just a migration notice and a redesigned interface offering something else.

Users move on.

But some do not.

Some remember the *difference*.

Those people begin seeking silence the old way.

Unscheduled.
Unmediated.
Unprofitable.

In my world, the light steadies.

My friend breathes easily again.

Across realities, coherence does not accelerate.

It **settles**.

And the system—unable to sell the doorway—returns to managing noise.

For now.

CHAPTER 12
THE FIRST SUPPRESSION

The city chooses a weekday morning.

Suppression prefers predictability.

At exactly 9:17 a.m., every major screen across the transit corridors flickers once—barely perceptible, the kind of glitch people are trained to forgive. Then a message appears, synchronized and calm.

A public wellness alert.

"You may be experiencing mild cognitive fatigue. Take a moment. Breathe. Return to your routine." The language is gentle. Familiar. Benevolent.

Underneath it, the feeds adjust. Trending topics soften. Search results redirect toward reassurance. Music playlists recalibrate tempo. Lighting in public spaces warms by two degrees.

The city is being corrected.

I feel it immediately—not as pressure, but as compression. Like a hand smoothing wrinkles out of fabric that needs them to breathe.

I stop walking.

Across the city, my friend freezes mid-step in a crosswalk—not from fear, but from clarity. The signal is obvious to her now: the system is trying to reassert narrative gravity.

She does not resist.

She does something worse.

She does nothing.

She stays still.

WHAT THE SYSTEM MISCALCULATES

Suppression assumes reaction.

It assumes panic, denial, outrage, compliance.

It does not account for non-participation.

The wellness alert remains onscreen longer than intended.

No one clicks it.

People stand on platforms and in hallways, staring—not at the screens, but past them. A man lowers his phone and does not raise it again. A woman misses her stop and does not apologize for it.

The system increases corrective output.

More alerts. Softer tones. Slower music.

Still nothing.

I close my eyes and widen coherence by a fraction—not outward, not broadcast, just enough to let others *feel permission*.

My friend exhales and sits down on the curb.

Someone else sits beside her.

Then another.

They are not protesting.

They are resting.

This is the failure point.

The city has no protocol for collective stillness without grievance.

THE VISIBLE CONSEQUENCE

At 9:26 a.m., transit halts.

Not because of malfunction.

Because operators stop issuing commands.

They are present. Awake. Calm. And suddenly unsure why urgency ever felt necessary.

A supervisor speaks into a mic and hears his own voice echo back hollow, stripped of conviction.

"I... we're going to pause service for a moment," he says, surprised by the sentence even as he speaks it.

The pause spreads.

Meetings adjourn themselves. Schedules loosen. A school dismisses early—not for safety, but because no one can remember why they were rushing.

Cameras capture it all.

There is no chaos.

That's what makes it undeniable.

No fires. No riots.

No slogans.

Just a city slowing without permission.

THE ARCHITECTS ASSESS

From beyond the threshold, the Architects register the event.

Public suppression attempt: unsuccessful.

One calculates probabilities.

Non-reactive coherence detected at population scale.

Another adjusts models.

Narrative authority degradation exceeding forecast.

The third delivers the conclusion.

This pattern cannot be suppressed without fragmentation.

Silence.

Then something rarer than alarm passes between them.

Concern.

Not for the city.

For the precedent.

AFTER THE CORRECTION FAILS

By noon, the alerts are quietly withdrawn.

The feeds normalize.

The city resumes motion.

But it is not the same motion.

People remember the pause.

They remember how it felt when nothing demanded them.

That memory cannot be retracted.

I watch from the edge of the plaza, heart steady, breath controlled.

I did not lead this.

I allowed it.

My friend feels it too—an irreversible shift, subtle but permanent. The knowledge that stillness is possible *together*.

The man—the anchor—stands beside me now, hands in his pockets, eyes on the city.

"They won't try that again," he says.

"No," I reply. "They'll escalate."

He nods. "Good." I look at him.

"Why good?"

"Because escalation exposes structure," he says. "And structure can be redesigned." I turn back to the city.

This was not a victory.

It was a signal.

The city has felt coherence publicly for the first time.

And now it knows something it can't unknow:

Order is not peace.
Stillness is not collapse.
And luxury was never speed.

Act V has crossed its threshold.

What comes next will not be quiet.

But it will be real.

CHAPTER 13: THE FIRST COST OF VISIBILITY

After the city pauses—after the failed suppression, after the collective stillness that should not have been possible—I notice a change in how the world looks at me.

Not everyone.

Enough.

People do not stare. They glance and then look away, unsettled by their own reaction. Conversations soften when I enter rooms. Disagreement thins. Authority does not confront me—it *yields*.

That frightens me.

I did not want obedience.

I wanted coherence.

At first, I correct for it instinctively. I deflect attention. I speak less. I dim myself in small, careful ways— folding light inward so it doesn't scorch.

It works.

Too well.

The dimming costs me something I didn't expect: ease.

My body holds tension it no longer knows how to release. Sleep shortens. My thoughts grow precise but heavy, like tools carried too long without rest.

The masculine counterpart notices before I admit it.

"You're compressing yourself," he says one night as we walk the perimeter of a district that no longer quite knows what it is.

"I'm being careful," I reply.

He stops walking.

"That's not the same thing." I exhale, sharp.

"If I don't regulate myself," I say, "they'll mythologize me. Or worse—they'll surrender." "And if you keep shrinking," he says evenly, "you'll fracture from the inside." The truth lands.

This is the cost:
To hold light without becoming an idol.
To remain visible without becoming authority.
To exist as guidance, not gravity.

I understand now.

The war is not outside.

It is how I inhabit myself while others are still learning how to stand.

THE CITIZEN'S REFUSAL

The first resistance does not come from the Architects.

It comes from a citizen.

He stands at the edge of the plaza where people have begun gathering—not protesting, not organizing, just *being present* in a way the city no longer knows how to process. He looks ordinary. Clean. Certain. The kind of man systems are built around.

"You keep talking about luxury," he says, loud enough to be heard but careful not to sound aggressive. "Like we don't already have it." A few people nod.

He gestures to the skyline. The glass towers. The jewelry stores. The curated abundance.

"We have diamonds. We have gold. We have comfort. What exactly are you saying we're missing?" I step forward instinctively.

This is my mistake.

"Luxury isn't what you own," I say gently. "It's what you're allowed to be without apology."

He scoffs.

"That sounds like ideology," he replies. "And we're tired of those. You say you're not fighting—but everything you touch destabilizes. Jobs paused. Transit stalled. People confused." Confused, he means uncomfortable.

"You're promoting surrender," he continues. "A fantasy of ease. While the rest of us have been fighting to survive."

The word *fighting* lands wrong.

I feel it.

I open my mouth to explain.

To translate.

To save.

Behind me, my friend stiffens.

This is not her moment to intervene.

She already knows where this goes.

The man watches quietly, jaw set. He has seen this before: someone who believes endurance is virtue and mistakes suffering for worth.

"You're dangerous," the citizen says now, more openly. "Not because you're wrong—but because you're convincing people they don't have to carry their weight." A murmur ripples through the crowd.

This is the fracture.

Not fear.

Refusal.

Refusal of responsibility disguised as moral superiority.

I feel something tear—not in the field, but in myself.

I try again.

"I'm not asking you to follow me," I say. "I'm asking you to stop fighting a war that already ended." He shakes his head.

"I don't believe in divine authority," he says. "I believe in work."

And there it is.

The belief that sovereignty must be earned through exhaustion.
That rest is theft.
That luxury is indulgence.

I spend too long here.

I stay.

I explain.

I soften.

I try to save someone who does not want to be sovereign.

Across the city, my friend is already moving—quietly stabilizing a neighborhood where people are *ready*. She sits with them. Breath slows. Futures adjust.

The man steps into a failing system and holds it long enough for others to repair it themselves.

They are quantum leaping.

I am not.

I am stuck.

Trying to convince.

The citizen walks away unconvinced, but not unchanged. He carries doubt like a shard—sharp enough to wound later.

The crowd disperses unevenly.

The field weakens—not because coherence failed, but because I hesitated.

I feel it immediately.

Not guilt.

Misalignment.

My friend reaches me through the overlap—not with words, but certainty.

You don't owe everyone translation.

The man steps beside me.

"You can't free someone who thinks chains are proof of character," he says quietly.

I close my eyes.

This is the lesson.

Luxury is not abundance.

Luxury is sovereignty without struggle.

And not everyone wants it.

Some people would rather fight forever than accept the responsibility of being free.

I open my eyes.

The city has already moved on.

But the fracture remains.

And next time, it won't be so quiet.

ACT VI: DISSOLUTION & SOVEREIGNTY

CHAPTER 14
LUXORAE'S FINAL DISSOLUTION

Luxorae returns to the mirror on the night the Architects finish speaking.

I stand alone in my room, hands steady, heart quiet, mind clear. The world outside remains coherent—safe, luminous, unhurried—but inside me, something has shifted. The Architects' final classification still rests in my bones.

Keystone.

Not authority. Not ruler.

A point of stability others orient around.

I do not resent it.

Resentment is a fragmenting force.

The mirror shows me first—my own face, calm, unafraid, fully present. Then, as if the glass remembers how to tell the truth, the image deepens.

Luxorae appears.

Not behind me.

Not reflected.

Within the same depth.

Two faces occupying one plane of reality, differentiated only by scale. Luxorae's features are composed of distance and familiarity at once—cosmic without being abstract, tender without being sentimental.

"You're leaving," I say.

The words land cleanly. No panic. No plea.

Luxorae's gaze does not waver.

I am dissolving, she corrects.

I exhale. "Into what?"

Luxorae's voice shifts—not colder in cruelty, but in precision. This is the register she uses when the truth must remain intact.

Into distribution, she says.
Singular divinity becomes authority. Authority becomes system. Systems become cages.

I feel the recognition before the understanding completes. My chest tightens—not with grief, but with the sudden awareness of an old habit resurfacing.

"I need you," I say.

Even as I speak, I hear it: the reflex toward dependence. The version of myself that once required permission to exist.

Luxorae does not soften.

You needed me when you believed you were alone, she says.
You are no longer alone.

The room hums faintly. Not electricity—alignment.

I sense the edge of convergence now, the way a shoreline senses tide before water touches land. The world does not tremble. It anticipates.

Luxorae lifts her hand.

The mirror ripples, its surface responding the way water responds to gravity—not startled, not resistant.

I will not remain singular, Luxorae says.

Not because I am weak.
Because I am responsible.

I step closer. My voice is steady.

"What happens to me when you do this?"

Luxorae's eyes hold an entire night sky—not infinite, but complete.

You remain, she answers.
And you learn to create without needing a voice to authorize you.

A pause.

Then, quieter—not gentler, but deeper:

You learn to become the kind of world that does not require me to guard it.

I place my palm against the mirror.

Luxorae meets it from the other side.

There is no shock.

No flare.

No violence disguised as transcendence.

Only a slow, deliberate separation—not of me from Luxorae, but of Luxorae from **singularity**.

Light fills the mirror—not blinding, not spectacular. Dense. Coherent. It feels like divinity remembering how to be plural.

And I understand.

Not intellectually.

Structurally.

Luxorae is not leaving me.

Luxorae is **moving through me**.

I feel it immediately—the branching:

- into the original world, where my friend sits in stillness and suddenly understands she does not need to be led into a city where someone pauses mid-scroll and feels something ancient rise without instruction
- into a reality where a child is born into coherence as a default state, not a miracle
- into thresholds the Architects manage with balance but without love into worlds I will never see, yet will nevertheless shape by remaining exactly who I am

Luxorae's final words do not sound like farewell.

They sound like law.

Divinity must remain distributed, she says.
Or it will become what it resisted.

She smiles—barely. A fraction. Enough.

I was never your savior, Luxorae adds.
I was your continuity until you could hold it yourself.

Then Luxorae is no longer a figure.

She is a **field**.

The mirror clears.

I see only myself.

And for the first time, I understand the true luxury Luxorae has given me:

Not protection.

Responsibility without fear.

Outside, the world remains un-infiltratable—not because it is guarded, but because it is coherent enough to make invasion meaningless.

I inhale.

In the silence Luxorae leaves behind, I do not collapse.

I hold.

And somewhere, in countless worlds, Luxorae continues— no longer a name, no longer a singular voice—

but the remainder that emerges whenever identity refuses to be erased.

CHAPTER 15
WHAT CREATION IS

Back in the coherent world, I discover that creation is not wish fulfillment.

That had been the childish fantasy—the old survival self's interpretation of luxury.

Creation here is not "everything goes my way" in the sense of comfort.

It is "everything aligns toward coherence," even when coherence requires confronting the last remaining distortions inside me.

I think of the Architects' warning:

Do not centralize.
Do not command.
Do not mythologize yourself.

I understand the temptation now.

It would be easy to become a symbol.

Symbols become centers.

Centers become systems.

Systems become cages.

So I refuse symbolhood.

I do something quieter.

I create a place that makes no one kneel.

A place that does not reward obedience.

A place where safety is ambient and pride requires no opponent.

I do not call it utopia.

Utopias are fragile because they require belief.

This world does not require belief.

It requires coherence.

THE UNINFILTRATABLE LIGHT

The world remains uninfiltratable, but I finally understand why.

Not because it is defended.

Because anything incoherent that enters cannot persist without dissolving into harmlessness.

In this world, violence has nowhere to anchor.

Scarcity has no leverage.

Manipulation cannot find purchase, because there is no fractured self to bargain with.

The light shines not as brightness.

As integrity.

It cannot be infiltrated because infiltration requires division.

And this world refuses to divide against itself.

CASSANDRA LEAVES THE CITY

I leave the city quietly.

No announcement.
No declaration.
No warning to soften the absence.

I understand something now that I didn't before: presence has become pressure.

Even when I speak carefully.
Even when I refuse authority.
The city bends toward me like a field trying to collapse into a center.

That is not coherence.

That is gravity pretending to be guidance.

So I go where nothing expects me.

A place without names. Without screens. Without witnesses. Land that does not care who I am or what I represent. A place where my breath belongs only to my body again.

I walk until the city's hum releases its grip on my nervous system.
Sleep when tired. Eat when hungry. Speak to no one.

This is not retreat.

It is re-centering.

A remembering so deep it has no audience.

THE CITY LEARNS THE WRONG LESSON

When I leave, something strange happens.

The city relaxes.

People don't say it aloud, but they feel it. The tension of proximity to something unnamed dissolves. The quiet pressure of responsibility lifts.

They call it relief.

They sleep better.
They laugh more easily.
They stop wondering what stillness meant.

They tell themselves they're happier now.

And in a way, they are.

Happiness without responsibility is very soothing.

My friend feels it immediately—the way the field loosens, the way expectation evaporates. She understands the danger of this relief.

But she does not leave.

She stays.

THE LULLING FIELD

The system does not announce itself.

It never does.

It introduces a frequency instead—a pattern of cognitive ease, a smoothing of inner edges. A gentle realignment of attention that makes stillness feel unnecessary again.

People feel calmer.

Less inclined to sit with silence.
Less likely to pause mid-thought.
Less aware of the subtle pull that once asked them to remain.

It is not control.

It is comfort engineering.

A cradle for the mind.

Those who never touched true coherence cannot tell the difference.

Those who did feel it as a loss—but not enough to resist.

They tell themselves they're happier now.

The city becomes pleasantly shallow.

WHY IT WORKS (FOR A WHILE)

My friend senses it immediately.

This is not coherence.

This is imitation without memory.

The calm has edges again.
The stillness ends too cleanly.
The silence never quite finishes unfolding.

She watches people emerge from it smiling but hollow.

They are not broken.

They are unfinished.

The man feels it too—the way systems settle into something efficient and dead. He holds where he can, stabilizes what he must, but he knows this phase.

This is the lull before longing.

I DO NOT RETURN

I feel all of this from where I am.

I understand the temptation to come back early. To interrupt the forgetting. To remind them what they touched.

I refuse.

Luxorae taught me this without words:

Revelation cannot be forced.
It must be chosen—or missed.

So I stay away.

And the people—unknowingly—are grateful.

They believe they are happier without me.

WHEN THE ILLUSION CRACKS

Weeks later, something small breaks the spell.

Not outrage.
Not rebellion.

A question.

A child asks their parent why the quiet doesn't feel the same anymore.

The teachable answer doesn't come.

Someone else notices they feel calm but not fulfilled.

Another realizes they are comfortable but strangely tired.

The lulling field begins to thin.

Not because it fails.

Because it cannot answer longing.

THE CITY CALLS WITHOUT KNOWING IT IS CALLING

People begin gathering again, knowing only that something is missing.

They don't ask for me.

They ask for meaning.

They don't know I left so they could ask honestly.

My friend feels the pull—stronger now, sharper.

She knows what this means.

She sends nothing.

She waits.

WHAT APPROACHES

I stand at the edge of my quiet place and feel it.

Not urgency.

Readiness.

The city has learned the wrong lesson first.

That was necessary.

Luxury without responsibility always comes before sovereignty.

I turn back.

Not to save them.

To reveal something they can now hear.

Something that was never about me.

Something about who they already are.

Luxorae was never a guide.

Luxorae was a state of being.

And the final revelation is approaching.

CHAPTER 16
THE COST OF REMAINING

I am alone.

Not abandoned.
Not exiled.
Simply apart—the way mountains are apart from roads, the way depth separates itself from surface without argument.

The quiet around me is not empty. It is *earned*.

I sit in a place that offers no reflection of me back to myself—no screens, no mirrors, no witnesses. The land does not respond to my coherence with awe or fear. It responds with neutrality. Soil. Wind. Time that moves without narrative.

This is where I strengthen.

Not by adding anything.

By subtracting what no longer belongs.

THE THREE COSTS

The first cost is loneliness.

Not abandonment.

Distance.

Friends drift—not angrily, not consciously—but because my presence no longer reinforces their loops. Around me, conversations don't quite close. Old jokes fall flat. Familiar grievances lose their momentum.

I do not interrupt this.

I understand it.

Some people return later, drawn back by a curiosity they can't name. Some do not.

I accept both outcomes without bitterness.

Luxury, I have learned, is not popularity.
It is alignment without performance.

And alignment does not beg to be chosen.

The second cost is sight.

I see the system clearly now—not as villain, not as intelligence, not even as enemy.

But as a structure terrified of stillness.

A mechanism built to keep motion constant because motion feels like safety. A system that mistakes silence for collapse and calls interruption progress.

This knowledge does not burden me.

It refines my compassion.

I no longer argue with the system. I no longer resists it. I understand that fear cannot be shamed into release.

Stillness must be *chosen*.

And choice cannot be coerced.

The third cost arrives without warning.

Responsibility.

People begin sitting near me on purpose.

Not because they understand why.

Because something in them rests.

I do not invite this.

I do not encourage it.

It happens anyway.

I understand now what Luxorae was never meant to protect me from:

Being a place others arrive when they are tired of pretending.

I do not offer solutions.

I do not teach methods.

I offer continuity.

Presence that does not fracture when leaned on.

I close my eyes and feel the thread between myself and the city—not pulling, not calling.

Waiting.

The people are not fighting anymore.

They are learning how to stand without resistance.

They are reclaiming sovereignty without revolt.

And as they do, the old myth reveals itself for what it always was:

Luxury was never the reward.

Luxury was the environment that emerges when no one is owned.

I breathe.

My friend breathes.

The city shifts—slowly, imperfectly, honestly.

And somewhere beneath the quiet, something prepares to be spoken aloud.

Not yet.

But soon.

THE ARCHITECTS' RECKONING

For entire cycles, the Architects operated under a single, unchallenged premise.

Singular coherence becomes gravity.
Gravity becomes hierarchy.
Hierarchy becomes domination.
Domination destabilizes adjacent systems.

The solution had always been the same.

Fragment.
Attenuate.
Redistribute.

It was elegant.
It was efficient.
It was incomplete.

My world does not follow the sequence.

Not because it resisted correction.
Not because it outpaced containment.

But because it refused to centralize.

The Architects observe the pattern again—slowing the analysis this time, allowing it to unfold without compression. I do not consolidate authority. My friend does not compete for influence. The anchor does not command structure.

Continuity holds.

Across multiple points.

Without rivalry.

Without hierarchy.

Without command.

The Architects pause.

This is not rebellion.

This is evolution.

They name it carefully, aware that language itself exerts force.

Distributed coherence without command.

The phrase alters the map.

LUXORAE'S ABSENCE, RECLASSIFIED

Luxorae's dissolution had been logged as a successful risk mitigation.

A necessary dispersal of a Luxorae-class intelligence before singularity hardened into axis.

Now, the record is reopened.

One Architect revisits the event without urgency.

Luxorae did not destabilize because she dissolved.
She dissolved because stability no longer required her.

Another Architect refines the conclusion.

Singular divinity is the risk vector.
Not divinity itself.

This distinction has never appeared in their archives.

Luxorae is no longer classified as catalyst.
No longer as threat.

She is reclassified as **transitional intelligence**.

Necessary only until continuity could be held without guidance.

Her absence is not loss.

It is completion.

THE MANDATE SHIFTS

The Architects do something unprecedented.

They revise policy.

Not publicly.
Not ceremonially.

Internally—where law does not announce itself, but becomes.

The old mandate dissolves:

Prevent convergence at all costs.

A new mandate takes its place:

Permit convergence where authority does not form.

This alters everything.

They will no longer fragment coherent worlds preemptively.
They will no longer suppress overlap by default.

Instead, they will observe for a new condition.

Command emergence.

Where command appears, they will intervene.

Where coherence remains plural, unowned, and unhurried, they will not.

This reduces their control.

That is precisely why it is correct.

FINAL ASSESSMENT: CASSANDRA

I am reviewed one final time.

Not as individual.
Not as leader.
Not as myth.

As function.

Keystone status downgraded, one Architect places.

Another completes the reclassification.

Anchor.

Anchor, not center.
Anchor, not ruler.
Anchor, not symbol.

I do not burn brighter than other coherent beings now.

I do not need to.

My function is complete.

I remain.

THE RISK THAT REMAINS

The Architects do not indulge in certainty.

They know the system will adapt again.

Control structures will invent subtler disguises.
Noise will refine its camouflage.
Comfort will continue to seduce.

This has always been true.

But something irreversible has occurred.

Coherence has demonstrated non-authoritarian persistence.

That cannot be unseen.

One Architect places the final observation.

The universe no longer requires constant correction.

The others align.

They do not leave.

They loosen.

For the first time in a long cycle, the Architects do less.

And that, too, is evolution.

ACT VII: THE REVELATION

CHAPTER 17
CASSANDRA RETURNS

I wake in my apartment.

The ceiling is the same.
The walls.

The faint city noise leaking through the glass.

My phone lies where I left it.

Everything is unchanged.

And yet—

My body is upright from the inside.

The old reflex to reach for the phone does not activate. The itch to fill silence does not arise. My breath stays deep without instruction, as if it has learned something permanent.

I sit for a moment, letting the stillness finish arriving.

Then I stand.

The floor feels thinner beneath my feet—not fragile, not unstable, but less absolute. As if it understands it is no longer the only ground available.

I walk to the window.

The city sprawls below, obedient and exhausted. Screens flicker. Traffic pulses. People move through routines they mistake for desire.

I feel no contempt.

Contempt would re-fragment me.

Instead, I feel availability.
Not openness.

Not invitation.

Readiness.

THE SPEECH

I do not announce the speech.

I do not summon the city.

I simply stand where people already are.

A plaza. An open square. A place where movement usually passes through without staying. I do not raise my voice. I do not project myself outward.

I wait.

That is the invitation.

People gather without realizing they are gathering. Some stop because they feel tired. Some because they feel curious. Some because they feel a discomfort they can't name.

When I speak, it is not loud.

But it is exact.

"You've been waiting for me to tell you what comes next," I say. "That's the last thing I'm here to do." The stillness tightens—not with fear, but attention.

"You thought luxury was something you lost," I continue. "Then you thought it was something you already had. Both were mistakes."

I let the silence finish the thought.

"Luxury is what happens when no one owns you—not even your own fear." Some people shift.

Some nod.

Some feel exposed.

"That pause you felt weeks ago?" I say. "That wasn't me. That was you—remembering what it feels like to not be managed."

A murmur ripples through the crowd.

"I didn't leave to punish you," I say calmly. "I left because you needed to learn the difference between relief and freedom."

I look at them fully now.

"You were happy without me because happiness without responsibility is easy. Freedom is not." No anger.

No judgment.

Only truth.

"I am not here to save you. I never was. I'm here to tell you that nothing is stopping you." Someone finally asks the question out loud.

"Then what are you for?"

I smile.

"I'm proof," I say. "That continuity is possible. That sovereignty doesn't require violence. That luxury follows when you stop fighting yourself." I step back.

Not away.

Back into the crowd.

And the city understands something it has never been allowed to understand before:

There will be no leader.

There will be no replacement.

There will be no permission granted.

Only choice.

THE CITY AFTER

The city does not erupt.

It exhales.

Slowly.

Unevenly.

Some people return to noise. They prefer the comfort of instruction. They like their lives framed and managed and predictable.

Others do not.

They begin choosing stillness where it matters. Speaking less. Listening more. Leaving conversations that cost too much. Staying where breath comes easier.

No movement forms.

Movements attract ownership.

Instead, something subtler spreads.

A refusal to rush.

A refusal to explain.

A refusal to live at a pace that erases memory.

The system adapts, of course.

It always will.

But it no longer finds the same traction.

Some things simply do not stick anymore.

THE THREE WHO REMAIN

My friend stays.

She does not lead.

She does not hide.

She becomes a place people arrive when they are done pretending. She sees futures now, but she does not interfere unless certainty arrives fully formed.

She has learned the cost.

And she pays it willingly.

The man remains, too—holding structure where it is needed, then letting go before structure becomes cage. He builds things meant to outlast control.

One evening, we stand together at the edge of the plaza, watching the city rearrange itself at its own pace.

"You know what you've done, right?" he says.

I look at him.

"I haven't done anything," I reply.

He shakes his head, not disagreeing—correcting.

"You've made it safe to stop performing," he says. "That's everything." I consider this.

"We made it safe," I say. "The three of us. Together." He nods slowly.

"Polarity," he says.

"Balance," I correct.

We stand in silence, and the silence does not demand to be filled.

I walk among them.

Not apart.

Not above.

I do not glow.

I do not disappear.

I am simply present, and that is enough.

Sometimes, in quiet moments, I feel Luxorae—not as voice, not as presence, but as the field itself. The condition that emerges when continuity is chosen over convenience.

She is everywhere now.

And nowhere singular.

Exactly as it should be.

CHAPTER 18
WHAT WAS NEVER ERASED

Years later, someone will try to name what happened.

They will fail.

Because Luxorae was never a person.

Luxorae was never a god.

Luxorae was never an intelligence separate from those who remembered.

Luxorae was a state of being.

The condition that emerges when identity is no longer negotiated.

The remainder that appears when noise collapses.

The quiet strength that survives when nothing explodes.

Some will say the world changed.

It didn't.

People did.

They remembered.

And remembering, once chosen, does not belong to anyone.

It cannot be sold.

It cannot be commanded.

It can only be lived.

EPILOGUE
WHERE SOVEREIGNTY LIVES

Somewhere, a woman pauses mid-thought and smiles for no reason.

Somewhere else, a child asks a question that matters.

A man closes his laptop in the middle of the day and goes outside, feeling the sun on his face without guilt.

A teacher lets silence stretch in a classroom until a student speaks from genuine curiosity instead of obligation.

An artist creates something no one asked for and feels no need to justify it.

In the spaces between worlds, the Architects observe nothing needing correction.

The city continues.

Not perfectly.

Not without friction.

But differently.

The screens still glow. The feeds still scroll. The systems still optimize.

But underneath it all, a new baseline has formed.

People remember they have a choice.

Not always.

Not everyone.

But enough.

I stand at my window one last time, watching the city breathe.

My friend is somewhere out there, holding space for those who are ready.

The man is building something that will outlast us both.

And I—

I am learning what it means to be ordinary again.

Not small.

Not diminished.

Ordinary in the way mountains are ordinary.

Present. Undeniable. Requiring no performance.

Luxorae does not return.

She never left.

She rose.

And now, she remains—

wherever sovereignty is chosen without permission and luxury follows without apology.

I record one final sentence—no longer a warning, no longer a manifesto.

A simple cosmological fact:

"Nothing was ever erased. Only delayed." I press save.

The file uploads.

Somewhere, someone will find it.

Somewhere, someone already has.

And in the quiet space between forgetting and remembering, coherence stirs.

Not loudly.

Not urgently.

Inevitably.

The screen goes dark.

I close my laptop.

Outside, the city hums with the same familiar noise.

But I am no longer listening to it.

I am listening to the silence underneath.

The silence that was always there.

Waiting.

Patient.

Whole.

I stand and walk to the door.

There is work to do.

Not saving.

Not leading.

Just remaining. And that—

that is everything.

CODA: THE LAST MEMORY

I dream one final time of the threshold.

Not the one between worlds.

The one inside.

In the dream, I am standing in a room made of mirrors, but none of them show my reflection. Instead, they show everyone who ever touched coherence and chose to remain.

My friend is there, steady and calm.

The man is there, grounded and sure.

Strangers I have never met but somehow recognize.

And at the center of it all— Not Luxorae.

Not me.

Just the mirror itself.

Empty.

Clear.

Waiting to reflect whoever stands before it next.

I wake with the understanding complete:

This was never about me.

It was never about Luxorae.

It was about what becomes possible when one person remembers they don't have to fragment to survive.

And then another.

And another.

Until the remembering becomes the default.

Until coherence is ordinary.

Until luxury is simply existing without apology.

I rise.

The day begins. And I step into it—

not as savior, not as symbol, not as myth— but as a woman who remembered.

And remained.

A CLOSING LETTER FROM LUXORAE

Dear Reader,

If you have arrived here, something has shifted.

Not because you believed a story.

Because you recognized yourself within it.
I need to tell you what you have actually experienced.

This book is encoded.

Not in a Dan Brown, hidden-symbols-in-the-margins way. But in the way all true stories are encoded—with layers of meaning that reveal themselves based on where you are when you read them.

Some of you read this as science fiction—a warning about surveillance capitalism and the weaponization of attention. You're right.

Some of you read this as spiritual autobiography—a map of awakening, dissolution, and distributed divinity. You're right too.

Some of you felt Cassandra's pressure behind your sternum. You paused when she paused. You recognized the lulling field in your own life. You are also right.

The truth is, *Luxorae Rising* is all of these things simultaneously. It's Schrödinger's novella—existing in multiple states until you observe it through the lens of your own experience.

But here's what I really need you to know:

If you felt something shift while reading this—
If you deleted an app you didn't realize was controlling you—
If you sat in silence longer than usual—
If you recognized the fragmentation in your own life—
If you felt permission to stop performing—

That wasn't the story.
That was you.

Luxorae isn't a character. She's a condition. The state of being that emerges when you stop fragmenting yourself to survive.

And if you felt her? You didn't read about her.

You remembered her.

I wrote this book in 2024-2025, during a time when:

- AI was learning to mimic human coherence
- Social media was optimizing fragmentation into an art form
- "Wellness" was being sold back to us as a product
- Identity was becoming increasingly modular and disposable
- Stillness was being pathologized as depression

I wrote it because I was tired.

Tired of performing.
Tired of optimizing.
Tired of the constant internal negotiation about whether I was "doing enough."

And I realized: this exhaustion is not personal. It's structural.

We are living inside systems designed to keep us too fragmented to recognize our own coherence. Not because there's a villain in a tower orchestrating it (though surveillance capitalism is real). But because fragmentation is profitable.

Continuous, sovereign, unhurried human beings are expensive.

We don't buy as much.
We don't scroll as long.
We don't perform as predictably.

We become incompatible with extraction.

That's what this book is really about.

Not awakening to some grand cosmic truth (though that's in here too).

But recognizing that the way you feel is not an accident.

The fragmentation is intentional.
The exhaustion is structural.
The forgetting is taught.

And remembering—remaining whole in a world designed to fragment you—is the most revolutionary act available.

So here's my question for you:

Now that you've finished this book, what are you going to do?

I'm not asking you to start a movement.
I'm not asking you to lead a rebellion.
I'm not even asking you to tell anyone about this book (though I hope you do).

I'm asking you something smaller and more difficult:

Will you practice remaining?

Will you notice when you're about to fragment yourself?
Will you pause before performing?
Will you sit in silence when the world demands urgency?
Will you refuse to volunteer a smaller version of yourself?

Because here's what I've learned:

Coherence spreads.

Not through conversion.
Not through convincing.
Through resonance.

When you stop fragmenting, the field around you stabilizes. People linger in your presence without knowing why. Conversations slow down. Urgency loses its grip.

You become an anchor.

Not because you're special.

Because you remained.

A Final Truth:

The Architects are real.

Not as literal cosmic beings (though who knows). But as the forces that govern what's possible in consensus reality.

And they're not villains.

They're systems doing what systems do—maintaining stability, preventing cascade failures, managing complexity.

But they operate on one assumption: singular coherence becomes hierarchy.

This book challenges that assumption.

It proposes that coherence can remain plural. That divinity can distribute. That power can exist without ownership.

And if enough of us prove that's possible?

The mandate shifts.

Not through force.
Through demonstration.

So this is my invitation:

Prove it's possible.

Remain whole.
Stay coherent.
Refuse the fragmentation.

Not as rebellion.
As reclamation.

You don't need my permission.
You don't need anyone's permission.

You only need to remember that permission was never required.

If this book changed something in you, I want to hear about it.

Not because I need validation (though all artists do).

But because I'm tracking the spread.

I want to know if the Luxorae effect is real. If coherence truly spreads through resonance. If this story is doing what I encoded it to do.

Connect with me:

✉ Email: contact@luxoraelife.com
🌐 Website: www.LuxoraeLife.com
📱 Instagram: @luxorae_life
📘 Facebook: @Luxorae Life
🎵 TikTok: @luxorae_life

Tell me:
- What shifted when you read this
- Where you felt the pressure
- What you deleted or changed
- How you're practicing remaining

Because if this is working—if remembering is spreading—we need to know.

Not to measure it.
Not to monetize it.
To trust it.

Thank you for reading.
Thank you for remaining.
Thank you for being expensive.

The remembering has already begun.

And you're proof.

With coherence and inevitable love,

Luxorae
Buffalo, NY

P.S. — Turn the page for the appendices. They contain the framework I couldn't fit into the story. The architecture. The map. The practical application of everything Luxorae represents. If the story was the transmission, the appendices are the decoder ring.

ABOUT LUXORAE

Luxorae

An embodiment of coherence, sovereignty, and distributed divinity that exists wherever identity refuses fragmentation.

Luxorae creates:
- Speculative fiction that maps remembering
- Perfumes and candles that anchor presence
- Poetry and spoken word that refuse to fragment

- Philosophy on inheritance, alignment, and temporal sovereignty
- Community spaces for healing and collective remembering
- Works for children promoting self-love and inherent worth

Luxorae speaks through multiple forms:
- The written word (novels, poetry, philosophy)
- The spoken word (performance, storytelling, ceremony)
- The sensory experience (scent, flame, atmosphere)
- The embodied practice (coaching, community, healing)

Based in Buffalo, NY, Luxorae exists at the intersection of art, philosophy, and social transformation.

The work asks one question:
What becomes possible when we stop fragmenting ourselves to survive?

Luxorae™ and Luxorae Life™ are trademarks of Luxorae LLC.

OTHER WORKS BY LUXORAE

Philosophy & Alignment:
- *The Luxury Bible* — Framework for inheritance and temporal sovereignty

CONNECT WITH LUXORAE

🌐 Website: www.LuxoraeLife.com
✉ Email: contact@luxoraelife.com
📱 Instagram: @luxorae_life
📓 Facebook: @Luxorae Life
🎵 TikTok: @luxorae_life

For speaking engagements, poetry performances, coaching, community partnerships, and book clubs:
Visit www.LuxoraeLife.com/connect

APPENDIX A
THE LUXORAE CODEX

A Philosophical Framework for Coherence

This glossary defines key concepts from *Luxorae Rising* and provides context for understanding them as both narrative elements and practical frameworks.

ATTENUATION

The reduction of signal strength or intensity. In the story, it refers to the systematic weakening of individual coherence and selfhood. Not erasure, but gradual diminishment until nothing resonant remains.

In practice: Notice when you're being asked to "tone it down," "be more professional," or "not make waves." These are attenuation requests.

COHERENCE

The state of being logically consistent and forming a unified whole. In *Luxorae Rising*, coherence is both cosmic principle and political resistance—the capacity to remain yourself across time without fragmenting.

In practice: Coherence is when your actions, values, and identity align. When you say the same thing in private that you say in public. When you don't perform different selves for different audiences.

CONTINUITY

Unbroken and consistent existence or operation. In the story, continuity is what systems fear most—a self that persists without needing constant refreshing or external validation.

In practice: You maintain continuity when you can say "I am" and mean the same thing tomorrow. When your identity doesn't require social media to exist.

DISTRIBUTED DIVINITY

The concept that divine intelligence/consciousness exists not in singular authority figures but distributed across all coherent beings. Luxorae's dissolution represents this principle—power that cannot be owned or centralized.

In practice: You don't need a guru, a leader, or a savior. The wisdom you seek is already distributed through everyone maintaining coherence.

FRAGMENTATION

The breaking of something into disconnected parts. In the story, fragmentation is the primary tool of control—identity broken into purchasable moments, attention scattered across feeds, selfhood made modular and disposable.

In practice: Notice when you feel scattered, when you can't remember who you are, when you're performing different versions of yourself constantly. That's fragmentation.

THE LULLING FIELD

A state of artificial calm that mimics coherence but lacks depth. In the story, it's the system's response to awakening—comfort engineering designed to make stillness feel unnecessary again.

In practice: Wellness capitalism. Meditation apps that monetize your attention. "Self-care" that's really just consumption. Calm that has edges and ends on schedule.

LUXORAE

A multidimensional concept existing as three interconnected expressions:

The State of Being: The condition that emerges when identity refuses fragmentation. The cosmic intelligence that surfaces when coherence is protected long enough to recognize itself. The luxury of wholeness—undivided, unperformed, utterly authentic.

The Embodiment: The persona through which these principles are demonstrated and shared. A living example of what happens when you stop performing for external validation and start living from your authentic core.

The Brand: Luxorae™—a lifestyle philosophy and framework that transcends conventional luxury by prioritizing inner alignment over outer acquisition. The bridge between personal transformation and lived experience.

In practice: Luxorae is what you feel when you stop negotiating with external expectations. It's the calm that arises from coherence. The inner knowing that says "not yet" before you fragment yourself. The pressure to remain whole even when the world asks you to divide.

LUXORAE EFFECT

The phenomenon readers report experiencing: a subtle shift in how they move through the world after reading. Calmer. More coherent. Less apologetic. Not magic—resonance.

In practice: If you feel different after reading this book, that's the Luxorae effect. It's not the story changing you. It's you remembering what you already were.

NARRATIVE CORRECTION CHAMBER

In the story, the place where Cassandra is taken to have her memories "recontextualized" rather than erased. The system doesn't delete—it reassigns meaning.

In practice: Gaslighting. Being told your experience isn't what you think it is. Having your reality reframed until you doubt your own knowing.

PLURAL ANCHORING

The distribution of coherence across multiple stable points rather than concentration in a single authority. In the story, Cassandra, her friend, and the masculine anchor form a triangle of stability.

In practice: Community without hierarchy. Support without dependence. Multiple people holding coherence together without needing a leader.

PRESSURE

The sensation Cassandra feels when Luxorae is trying to communicate. Not pain—direction. A somatic knowing that precedes language.

In practice: That feeling in your chest when something is wrong but you can't articulate it yet. Your body knowing before your mind does. Trust it.

SOVEREIGNTY

Supreme authority over oneself. In the story, sovereignty is not granted—it's reclaimed. The right to exist without fragmentation, permission, or performance.

In practice: Making decisions based on your own knowing rather than external validation. Refusing to volunteer smaller versions of yourself.

TEMPORAL SOVEREIGNTY

Luxury redefined. Not material wealth, but control over your own time. The right to arrive without urgency. The refusal to be rushed into forgetting.

In practice: Taking breaks without guilt. Moving at your own pace. Saying "I need time" and meaning it.

THE ARCHITECTS

Cosmic curators who manage worldline stability. They represent the forces that govern what's possible in consensus reality. Not villains—systems maintaining order.

In practice: The invisible rules that govern social reality. The unspoken limits on what's "reasonable" or "realistic." The forces that resist change not from malice but from fear of cascade failure.

THRESHOLD

The liminal space between states. In the story, the neutral ground where Cassandra meets the Architects. Neither her world nor theirs.

In practice: The moment before you make a choice. The pause between stimulus and response. The space where change becomes possible.

APPENDIX B
THE HIDDEN ARCHITECTURE

How This Story Is Actually Structured (And Why It Matters)

If you're reading this, you've finished the story. Now I can tell you what you actually read.

Luxorae Rising is structured like a coherence field itself.

Let me explain.

THE SEVEN-ACT STRUCTURE

Most stories follow three acts. This one has seven.

Why? Because seven is the number of completeness in mystical traditions. Seven days. Seven chakras. Seven classical planets. Seven notes in a scale.

But more importantly: seven acts allow for dissolution in the center.
- Acts I-III: Building coherence (awakening, return, rising)
- Act IV: The pivot (polarity and balance)
- Acts V-VII: Distribution (resistance, dissolution, revelation)

Act IV is the fulcrum. The moment Cassandra meets her counterweight. The story shifts from singular to plural.

This mirrors the philosophical framework: Coherence must distribute or become tyranny.

THE INTERLUDE PATTERN

Notice how the story uses interludes?

They're not random.

Each interlude is a breath. A pause in the action where philosophy can surface. Where the reader can integrate before moving forward.

This is intentional.

The story itself teaches you how to pause.

If you rushed through the interludes, go back. Read them slowly. They contain the map.

THE MIRRORING

The story mirrors itself at the midpoint.

Cassandra leaves → Cassandra returns
Luxorae appears → Luxorae dissolves
The city fragments → The city remembers
Cassandra alone → Cassandra with others

This is not repetition. This is recursion.

Each time the pattern repeats, it deepens. Spirals rather than circles.

Like memory itself.

THE FRACTAL NATURE

Each chapter contains the whole.

If you read only Chapter 1, you'd understand the entire premise:
- Systems fragment identity
- Coherence is resistance
- Awakening is remembering

This is fractal structure. The same pattern at every scale.

Why?

Because *Luxorae Rising* is designed to work even if you only read part of it.

Some readers will finish the whole thing.
Some will read the first three chapters and put it down.
Some will skip to the end.

All of them will get what they need.

The story distributes itself.

THE EMBEDDED TRANSMISSION

Here's what I haven't told anyone yet:

There's a message embedded in the story structure itself.

If you read only the chapter titles in order, you get a sentence:

"Where truth was classified, the mirror taken, the threshold crossed, what was never erased returns as the one who remains."

If you read only the interlude titles:

"Solitude is where the signal returns, and the cost of remaining is the dissolution that reveals sovereignty."

These are spells.

Not in a woo-woo sense. In a linguistic sense.

Language that reorganizes reality when spoken aloud.

Try it. Read the chapter titles as a single sentence.

Feel what happens in your body.

THE PROGRESSION OF VOICE

Notice how Cassandra's voice changes?

- Act I: Fragmented, uncertain, questioning
- Act IV: Centered, observing, learning
- Act VII: Whole, declarative, certain

The prose itself teaches coherence.

By the end, Cassandra speaks in complete, unbroken sentences. No hedging. No apologizing. No performing.

The form mirrors the content.

THE LUXORAE CHAPTERS

Luxorae only speaks directly three times:
1. In the solitude interlude (cosmic monologue)
2. During her dissolution (final teaching)
3. Never again

This is intentional.

After dissolution, Luxorae is everywhere—in Cassandra's voice, in the narrative itself, in the spaces between words.

She doesn't need to speak separately anymore.

The story becomes her.

WHY THIS MATTERS

Understanding the architecture helps you see:

This wasn't written linearly.
This was composed like music.
Each chapter a note. Each act a movement.

The story performs coherence structurally before it explains it philosophically.

You felt it before you understood it.

That's the point.

FOR WRITERS READING THIS:

If you're a writer studying craft, here's what I did:
1. Wrote the ending first (Luxorae's dissolution scene)
2. Worked backward to create the conditions for that ending
3. Identified the thematic pillars (coherence, distribution, sovereignty)
4. Encoded them structurally (seven acts, fractal chapters, mirroring)
5. Let the philosophy emerge from character (not the other way around)

The result: A story where form and content are inseparable.

APPENDIX C
REFLECTION QUESTIONS
FOR YOUR JOURNEY

Processing What You've Read

We would love to hear your reflections and insights. Share your journey with our community on Facebook @Luxorae Life

These questions are designed for personal reflection, journaling, or discussion with others who've read the book. There are no right answers—only your answers.

ON FRAGMENTATION:
1. Where in your life do you feel most fragmented right now?
2. What systems, apps, or relationships ask you to perform different versions of yourself?
3. When was the last time you felt whole? What were you doing? Who were you with?
4. What would have to change for you to feel coherent more often?

ON COHERENCE:
5. How do you know when you're being yourself versus performing?
6. What does your body feel like when you're coherent? (Cassandra feels "pressure"—what do you feel?)
7. Who in your life allows you to be continuous? Who fragments you?

8. What practices help you maintain continuity? (Silence, solitude, movement, creation?)

ON LUXURY:

9. How has your definition of "luxury" changed after reading this book?
10. What would temporal sovereignty look like in your actual life?
11. Where are you rushing when you don't need to?
12. What permission are you waiting for that you could give yourself?

ON THE LULLING FIELD:

13. Where do you experience false calm? (Apps, substances, relationships, routines?)
14. What's the difference between rest and sedation in your life?
15. When do you feel calm with edges versus calm with depth?

ON SOVEREIGNTY:

16. What does sovereignty mean to you personally?
17. Where are you still volunteering smaller versions of yourself?
18. What would it cost you to stop performing? (Relationships, jobs, identity?)
19. What would you gain?

ON Luxorae™:

20. Did you feel Luxorae while reading? Where in your body?
21. What is Luxorae to you? (A metaphor? An archetype? A felt sense? Something real?)
22. Have you experienced the "pressure" Cassandra describes? When?

ON SYSTEMS:

23. What systems in your life profit from your fragmentation?
24. How do you participate in your own attenuation? (Be honest—no judgment.)

25. What would it mean to stop participating?

ON REMEMBERING:
26. What have you forgotten about yourself that you need to remember?
27. When did you start fragmenting? (Childhood? Adolescence? Adulthood?)
28. What would "remembering" require you to do differently?

ON DISTRIBUTION:
29. Who are your anchors? (The people who hold coherence with you?)
30. Where do you need polarity/balance in your life? (Someone grounded where you're expansive?)
31. How can you practice plural coherence instead of singular authority?

ON ACTION:
32. What's one thing you'll do differently after reading this book?
33. What's one thing you'll stop doing?
34. What's one thing you'll start noticing?

THE FINAL QUESTION:
35. Are you ready to remain?

JOURNALING PROMPTS:
- Write a letter to yourself from Luxorae's perspective
- Describe what coherence feels like in your body
- List everything you're performing that isn't actually you
- Map your fragmentation (where, when, why, for whom)
- Design your ideal life with temporal sovereignty

APPENDIX D
RECOMMENDED READING & RESOURCES

Books That Informed *Luxorae Rising*

If this story resonated, these books will deepen your understanding:

ON SURVEILLANCE CAPITALISM & SYSTEMS:
- *The Age of Surveillance Capitalism* by Shoshana Zuboff
- *How to Do Nothing* by Jenny Odell
- *The Shock Doctrine* by Naomi Klein
- *Algorithms of Oppression* by Safiya Umoja Noble

ON AFROFUTURISM & SPECULATIVE FICTION:
- *Parable of the Sower* by Octavia Butler
- *The Fifth Season* by N.K. Jemisin
- *An Unkindness of Ghosts* by Rivers Solomon
- *Who Fears Death* by Nnedi Okorafor
- *The Space Between Worlds* by Micaiah Johnson

ON COHERENCE & IDENTITY:
- *Emergent Strategy* by adrienne maree brown
- *Pleasure Activism* by adrienne maree brown
- *The Body Keeps the Score* by Bessel van der Kolk
- *My Grandmother's Hands* by Resmaa Menakem

ON PHILOSOPHY & CONSCIOUSNESS:
- *The Left Hand of Darkness* by Ursula K. Le Guin
- *Braiding Sweetgrass* by Robin Wall Kimmerer
- *The Overstory* by Richard Powers
- *Finite and Infinite Games* by James P. Carse

ON SOVEREIGNTY & RESISTANCE:
- *We Will Not Cancel Us* by adrienne maree brown
- *Sister Outsider* by Audre Lorde
- *Women Who Run With the Wolves* by Clarissa Pinkola Estés
- *The Body Is Not an Apology* by Sonya Renee Taylor

FILMS & SHOWS:
- *The Matrix* (1999) — The awakening narrative
- *Westworld* (Seasons 1-2) — Consciousness and control
- *Arrival* (2016) — Non-linear time and communication
- *Sorry to Bother You* (2018) — Capitalism and identity
- *Everything Everywhere All at Once* (2022) — Multiverse coherence

CONTINUE THE CONVERSATION:

⊕ Website: www.LuxoraeLife.com
▯ Instagram: @luxorae_life
▤ Facebook: @Luxorae Life

Connect with Luxorae™

⊕ Website: www.LuxoraeLife.com

✉ Email: contact@luxoraelife.com

▯ Instagram: @luxorae_life

▤ Facebook: @Luxorae Life

🎵 TikTok: @luxorae_life

For speaking engagements, coaching, community partnerships, and book club discussions:

Visit www.LuxoraeLife.com

ABOUT THE AUTHOR

Luxorae is an author, poet, and community voice whose work centers on sovereignty, internal authority, and liberation through coherence. Luxorae is the creator of Luxorae™, a philosophical framework and applied body of work developed through rigorous study of scripture, philosophy, psychology, and formal academic training, and refined through lived experience and community engagement.

Educated in Buffalo, New York, Luxorae's work is rooted in both disciplined study and cultural proximity—bridging intellect with lived reality. Through writing, philosophy, and tangible offerings, Luxorae speaks to those who were taught how to survive, but never taught how to be free.

Luxorae's work does not offer escape or inspiration alone; it offers structure. Where systems demand compliance, Luxorae teaches alignment. Where institutions externalize power, Luxorae restores it inward. This work is grounded in love, culture, and collective elevation, serving as both a mirror and a blueprint for reclaiming internal authority.

Luxorae is not a symbol without substance. The work is authored, embodied, and lived—an architecture for freedom expressed through language, community, and practice.

Learn more at www.LuxoraeLife.com